MORE PRAISE FOR BABYMOUSE!

"Sassy, smart . . . Babymouse is here to stay."
—**The Horn Book Magazine**

"Young readers will happily fall in line."
—**Kirkus Reviews**

"The brother-sister creative team hits the mark with humor, sweetness, and characters so genuine they can pass for real kids." —**Booklist**

"Babymouse is spunky, ambitious, and, at times, a total dweeb."
—**School Library Journal**

Be sure to read **all** the **BABYMOUSE** books:

#1 BABYMOUSE: Queen of the World!
#2 BABYMOUSE: Our Hero
#3 BABYMOUSE: Beach Babe
#4 BABYMOUSE: Rock Star
#5 BABYMOUSE: Heartbreaker
#6 CAMP BABYMOUSE
#7 BABYMOUSE: Skater Girl
#8 BABYMOUSE: Puppy Love
#9 BABYMOUSE: Monster Mash
#10 BABYMOUSE: The Musical
#11 BABYMOUSE: Dragonslayer
#12 BABYMOUSE: Burns Rubber
#13 BABYMOUSE: Cupcake Tycoon
#14 BABYMOUSE: Mad Scientist

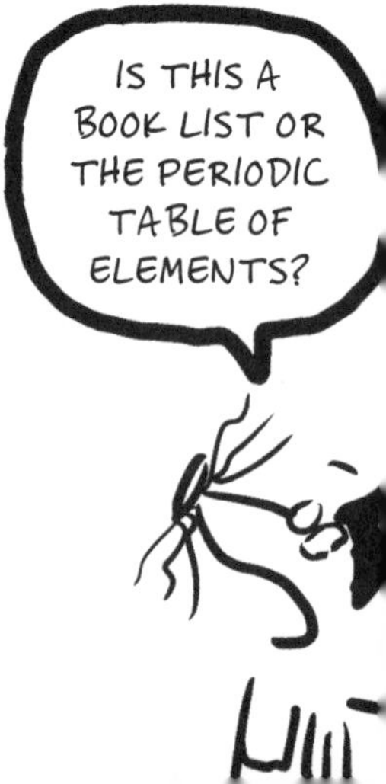
IS THIS A BOOK LIST OR THE PERIODIC TABLE OF ELEMENTS?

BABYMOUSE

MAD SCIENTIST

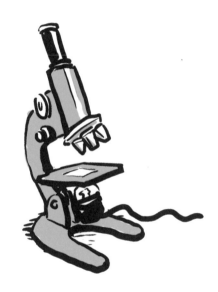

BY JENNIFER L. HOLM & MATTHEW HOLM

RANDOM HOUSE NEW YORK

$E = Books + Cupcakes^2$

IT'S THE THEORY OF BABYMOUSE!

Copyright © 2011 by Jennifer Holm and Matthew Holm

All rights reserved.
Published in the United States by Random House Children's Books, a division of Random House, Inc., New York.

RANDOM HOUSE and the colophon are registered trademarks of Random House, Inc.

Visit us on the Web! www.randomhouse.com/kids
Babymouse.com

Educators and librarians, for a variety of teaching tools, visit us at
www.randomhouse.com/teachers

Library of Congress Cataloging-in-Publication Data
Holm, Jennifer L.
Babymouse: mad scientist / by Jennifer L. Holm and Matthew Holm. — 1st ed.
   p. cm.
Summary: Babymouse discovers Squish, a new species of amoeba, while working on a school science fair project.
ISBN 978-0-375-86574-9 (trade) — ISBN 978-0-375-96574-6 (lib. bdg.)
I. Graphic novels. [1. Graphic novels. 2. Amoeba—Fiction. 3. Science projects—Fiction. 4. Schools—Fiction. 5. Mice—Fiction.] I. Holm, Matthew. II. Title.
III. Title: Mad scientist.
PZ7.7.H65Bag 2009 741.5'973—dc22 2009047388

MANUFACTURED IN MALAYSIA   10 9 8 7 6 5 4 3 2   First Edition

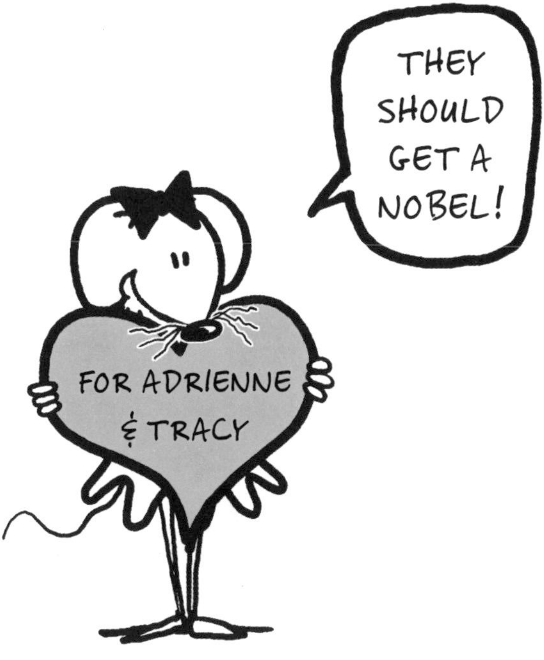
THEY SHOULD GET A NOBEL!
FOR ADRIENNE & TRACY

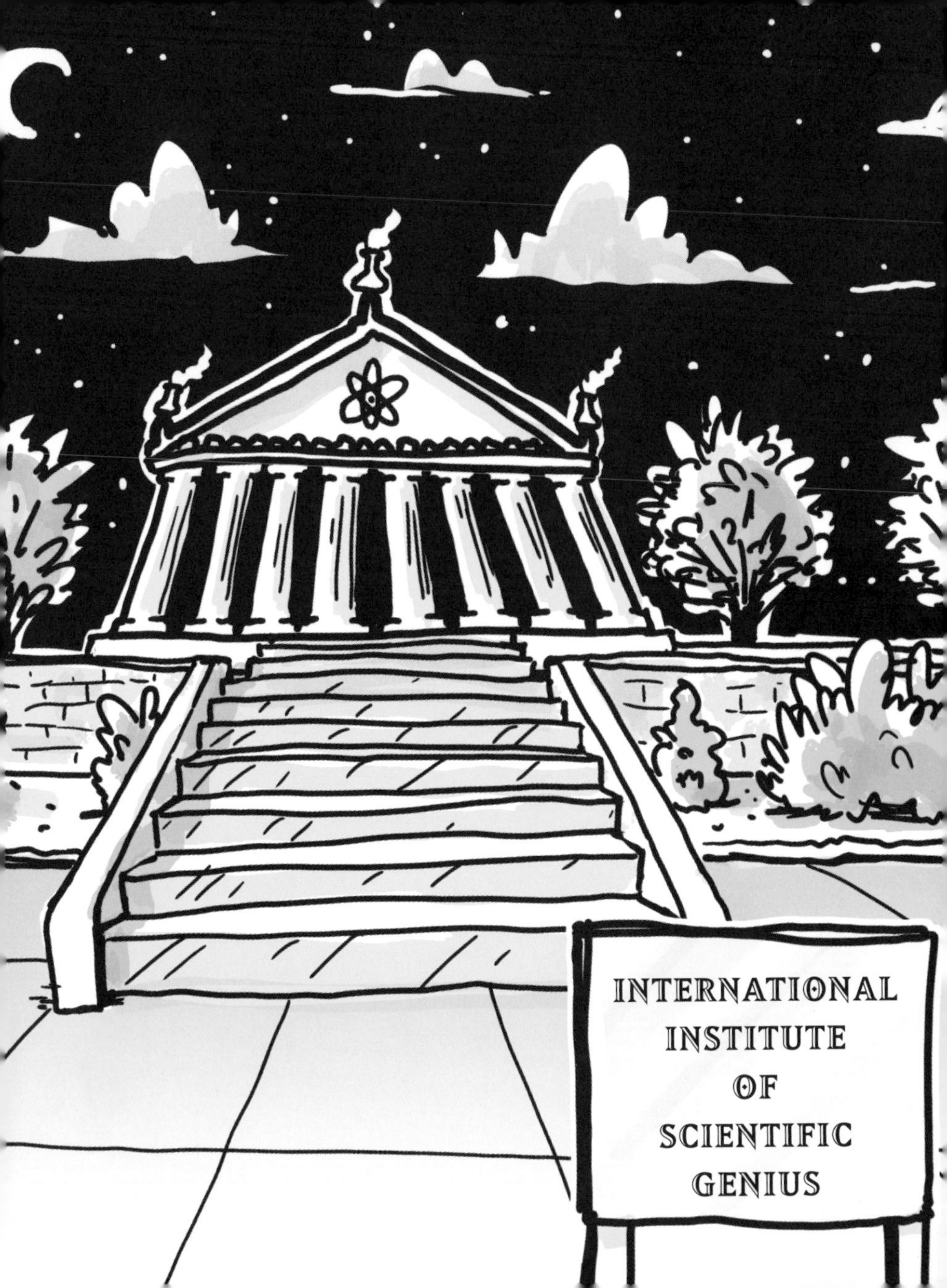
INTERNATIONAL
INSTITUTE
OF
SCIENTIFIC
GENIUS

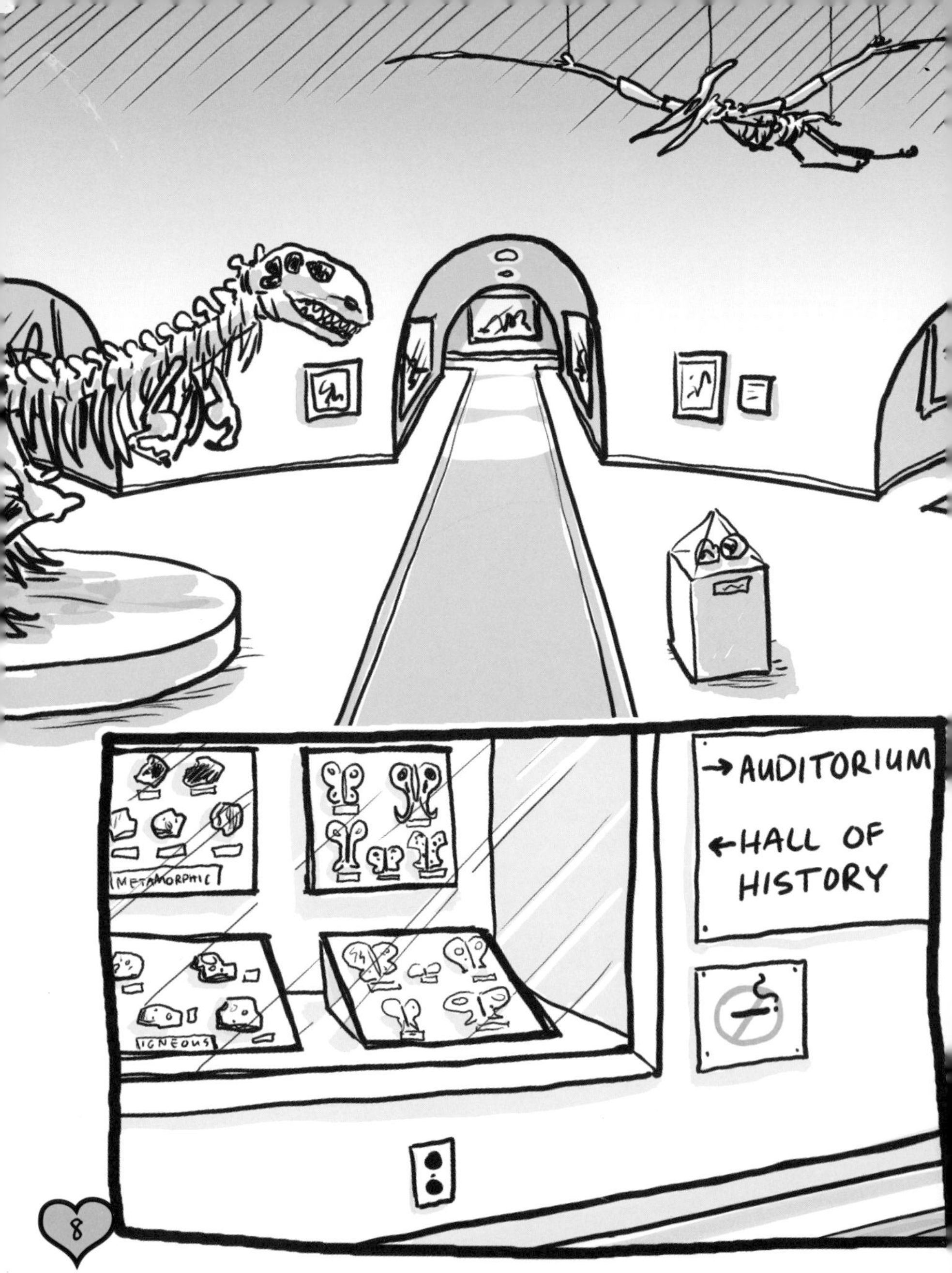
METAMORPHIC
IGNEOUS
→AUDITORIUM
←HALL OF HISTORY

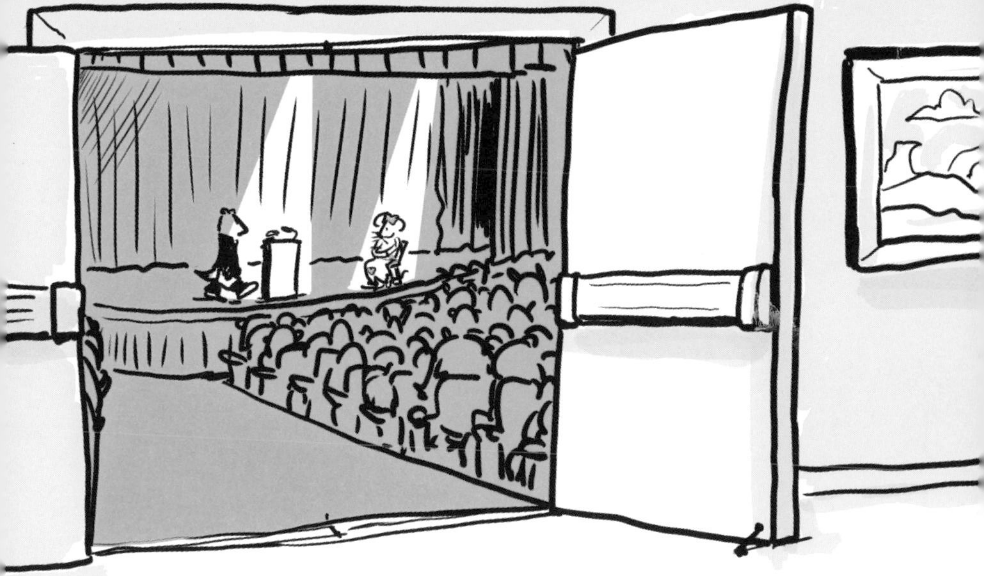

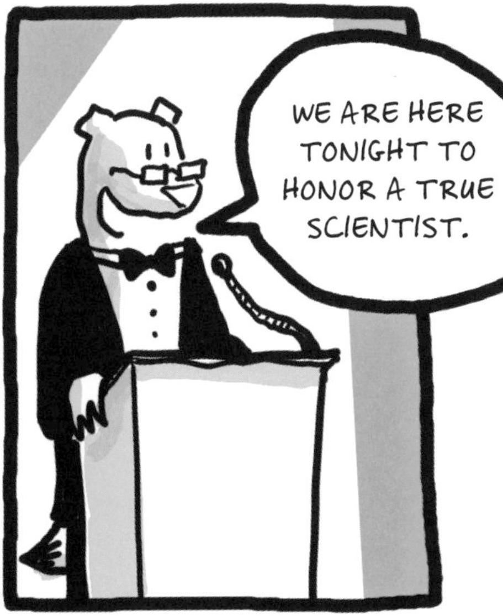
WE ARE HERE TONIGHT TO HONOR A TRUE SCIENTIST.

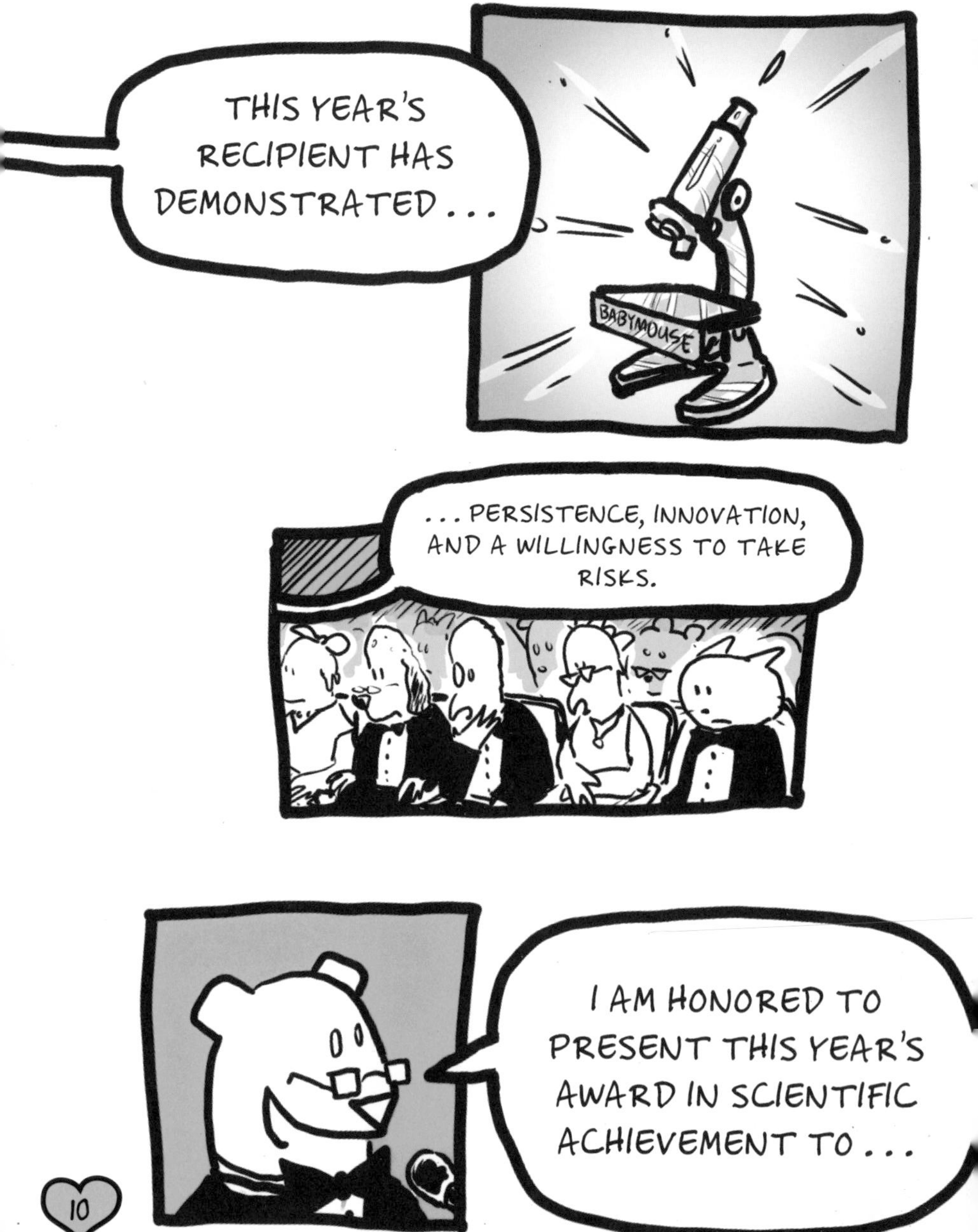
THIS YEAR'S RECIPIENT HAS DEMONSTRATED...
BABYMOUSE
...PERSISTENCE, INNOVATION, AND A WILLINGNESS TO TAKE RISKS.
I AM HONORED TO PRESENT THIS YEAR'S AWARD IN SCIENTIFIC ACHIEVEMENT TO...

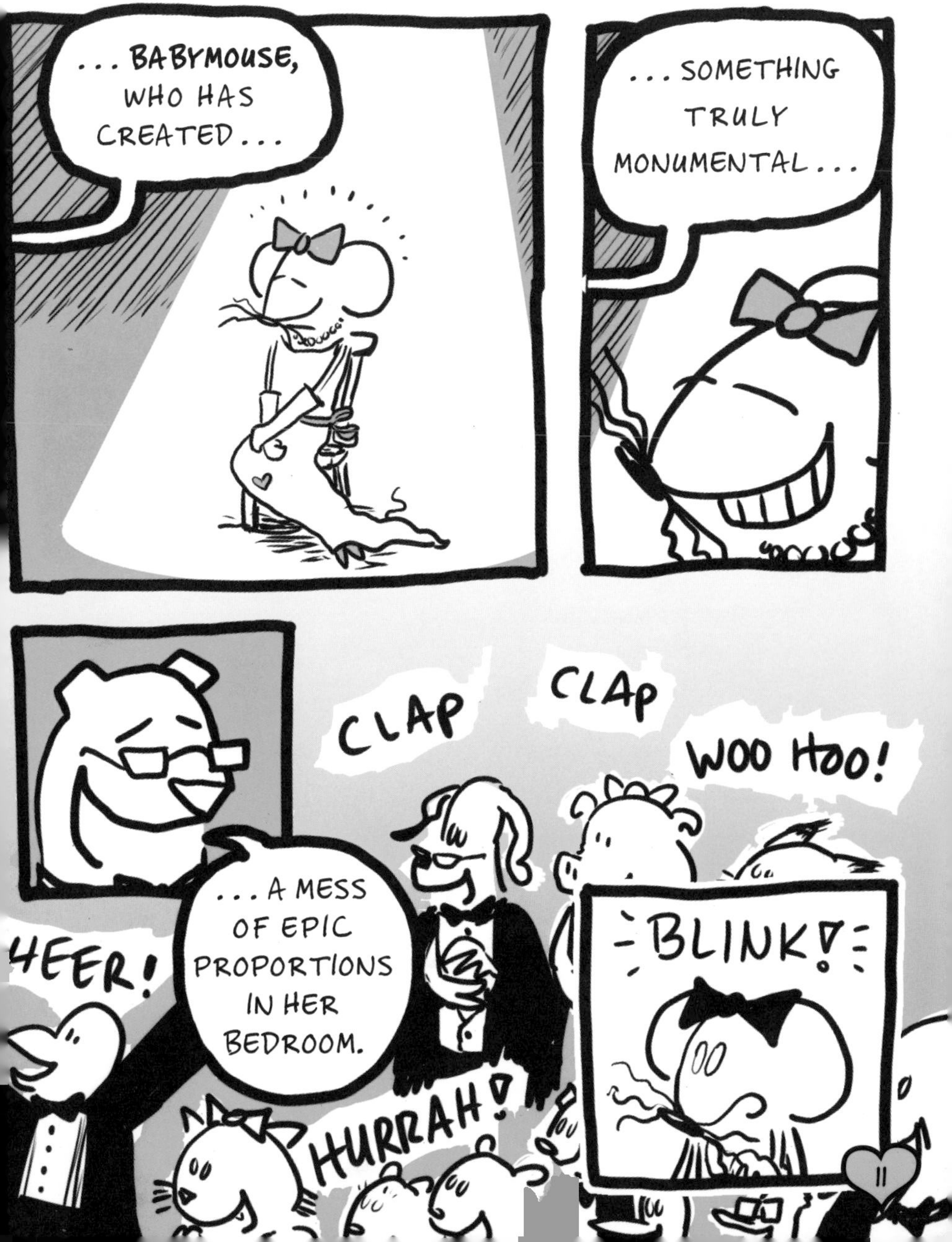

. . . BABYMOUSE, WHO HAS CREATED . . .
. . . SOMETHING TRULY MONUMENTAL . . .
. . . A MESS OF EPIC PROPORTIONS IN HER BEDROOM.
CLAP
CLAP
WOO HOO!
HEER!
HURRAH!
BLINK!

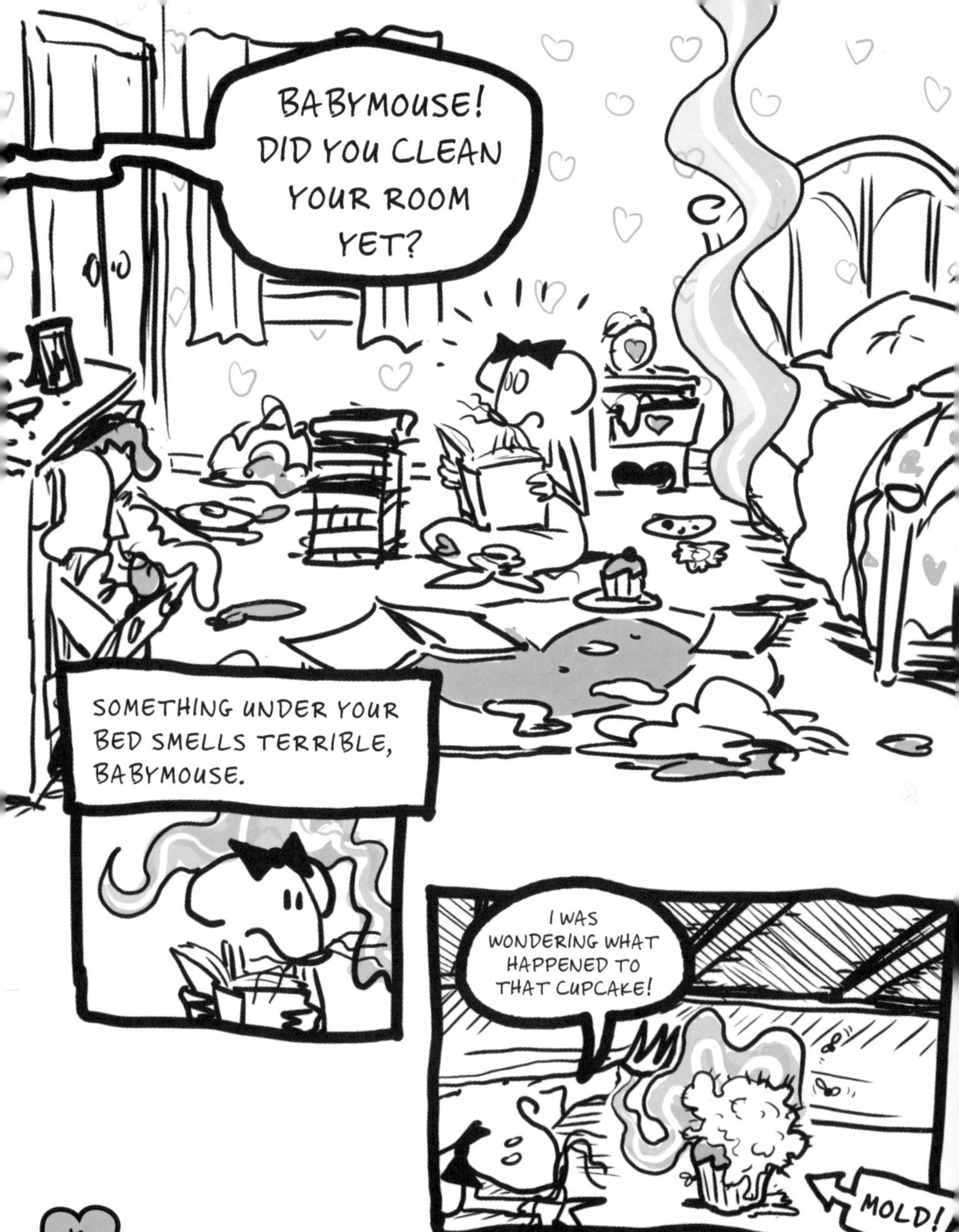
BABYMOUSE! DID YOU CLEAN YOUR ROOM YET?
SOMETHING UNDER YOUR BED SMELLS TERRIBLE, BABYMOUSE.
I WAS WONDERING WHAT HAPPENED TO THAT CUPCAKE!
MOLD!

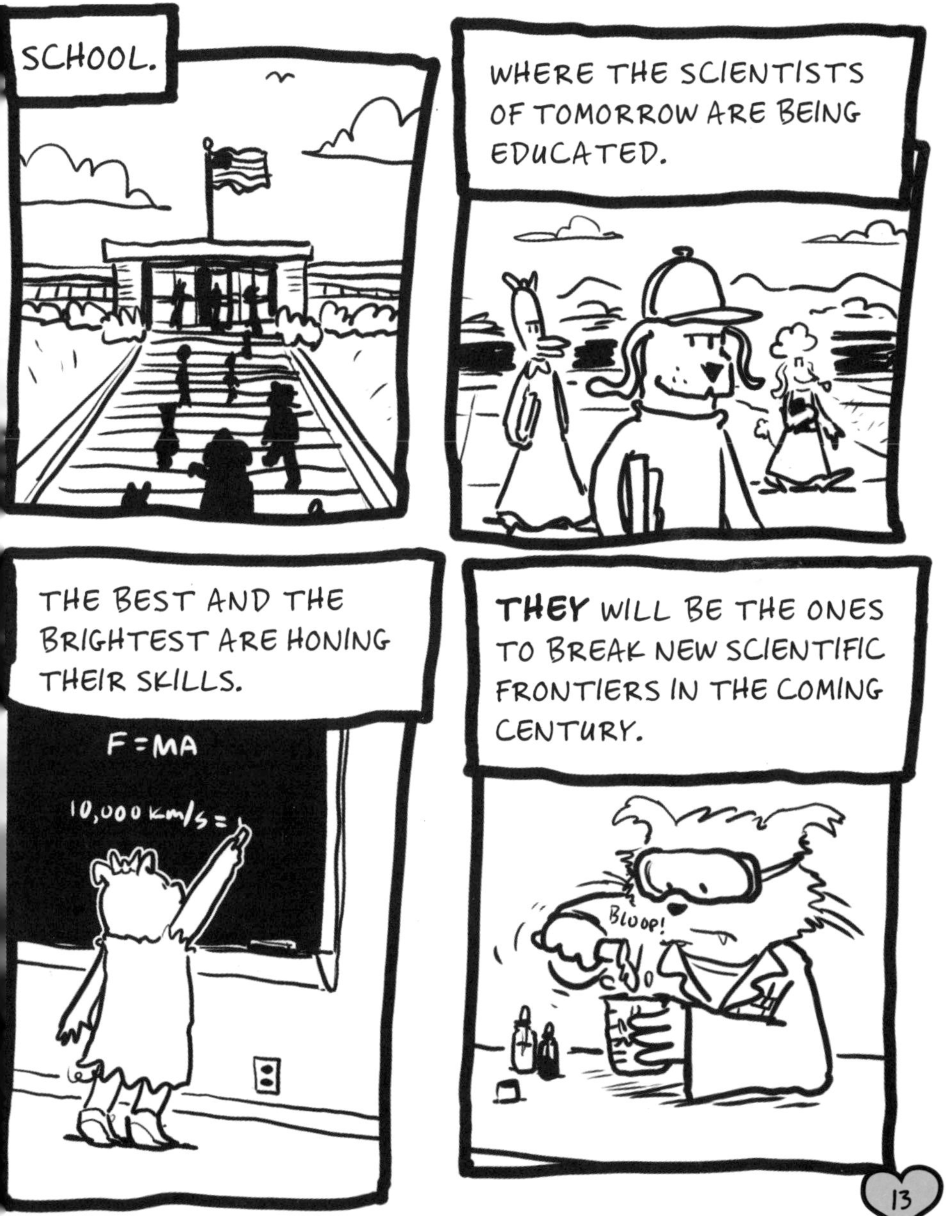
SCHOOL.
WHERE THE SCIENTISTS OF TOMORROW ARE BEING EDUCATED.
THE BEST AND THE BRIGHTEST ARE HONING THEIR SKILLS.
F=MA
10,000 km/s =
THEY WILL BE THE ONES TO BREAK NEW SCIENTIFIC FRONTIERS IN THE COMING CENTURY.
BLOOP!

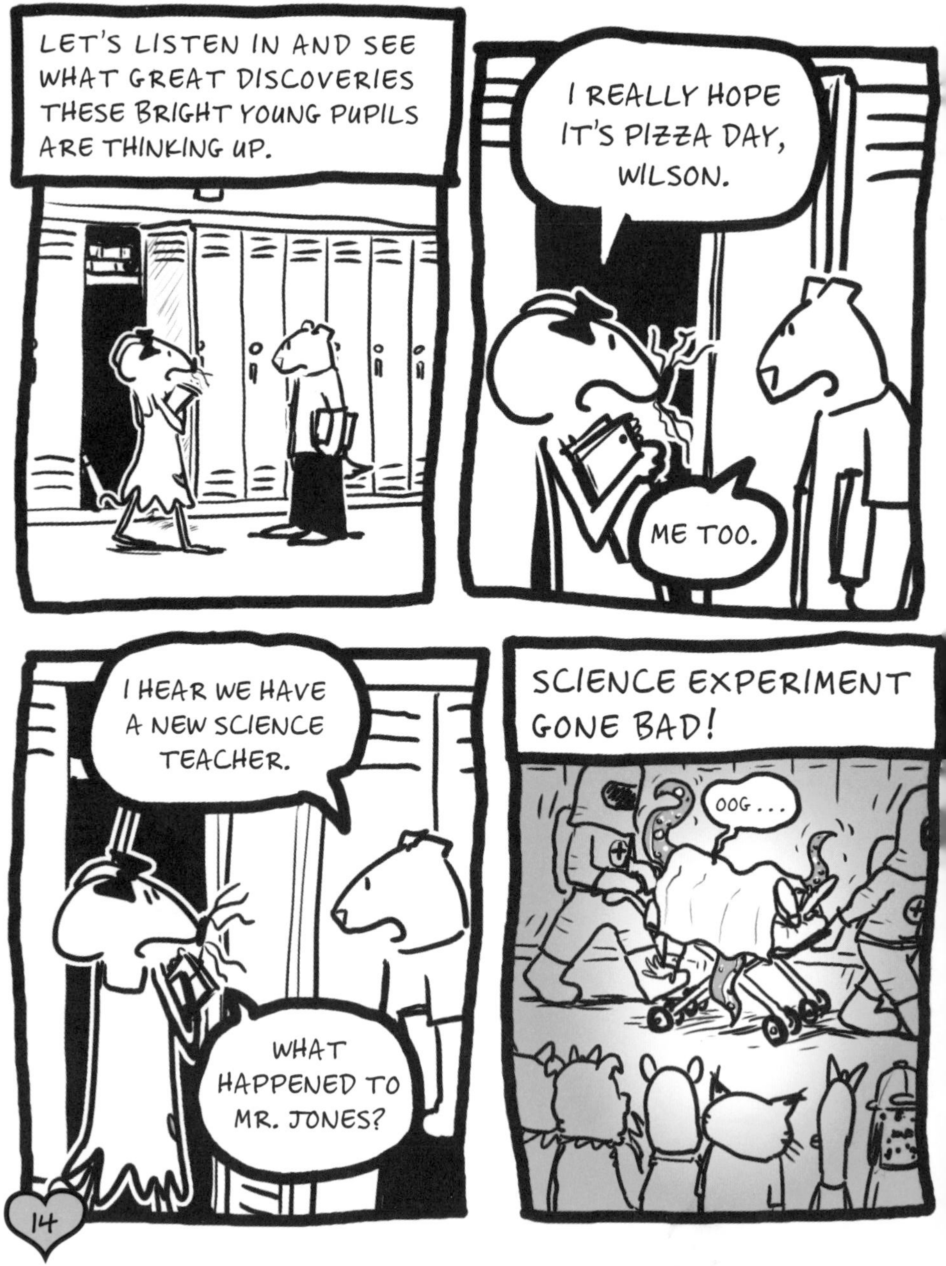
LET'S LISTEN IN AND SEE WHAT GREAT DISCOVERIES THESE BRIGHT YOUNG PUPILS ARE THINKING UP.
I REALLY HOPE IT'S PIZZA DAY, WILSON.
ME TOO.
I HEAR WE HAVE A NEW SCIENCE TEACHER.
WHAT HAPPENED TO MR. JONES?
SCIENCE EXPERIMENT GONE BAD!
OOG . . .

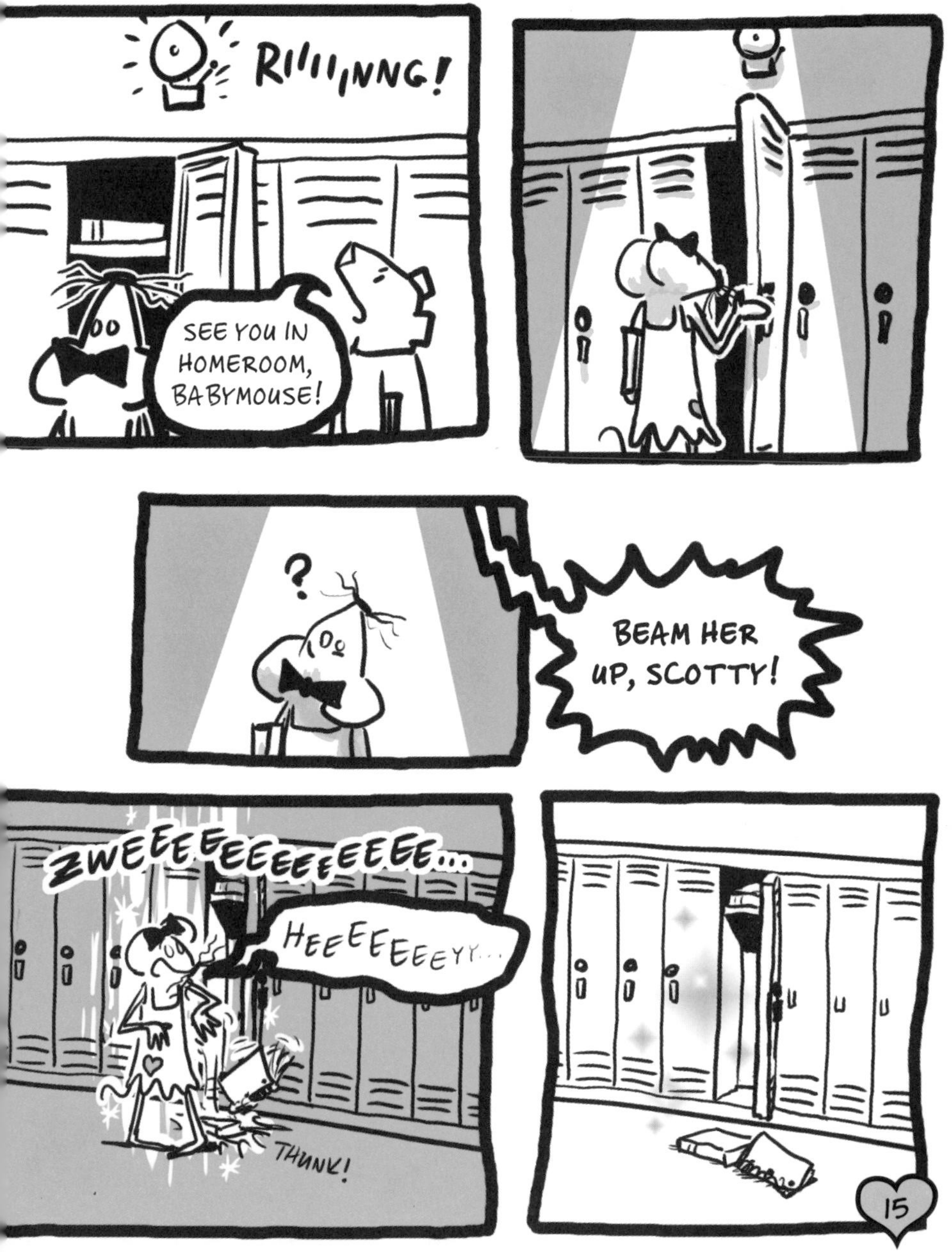
RIIIIINNG!
SEE YOU IN HOMEROOM, BABYMOUSE!
?
BEAM HER UP, SCOTTY!
ZWEEEEEEEEEEEEEE...
HEEEEEEEEYY...
THUNK!

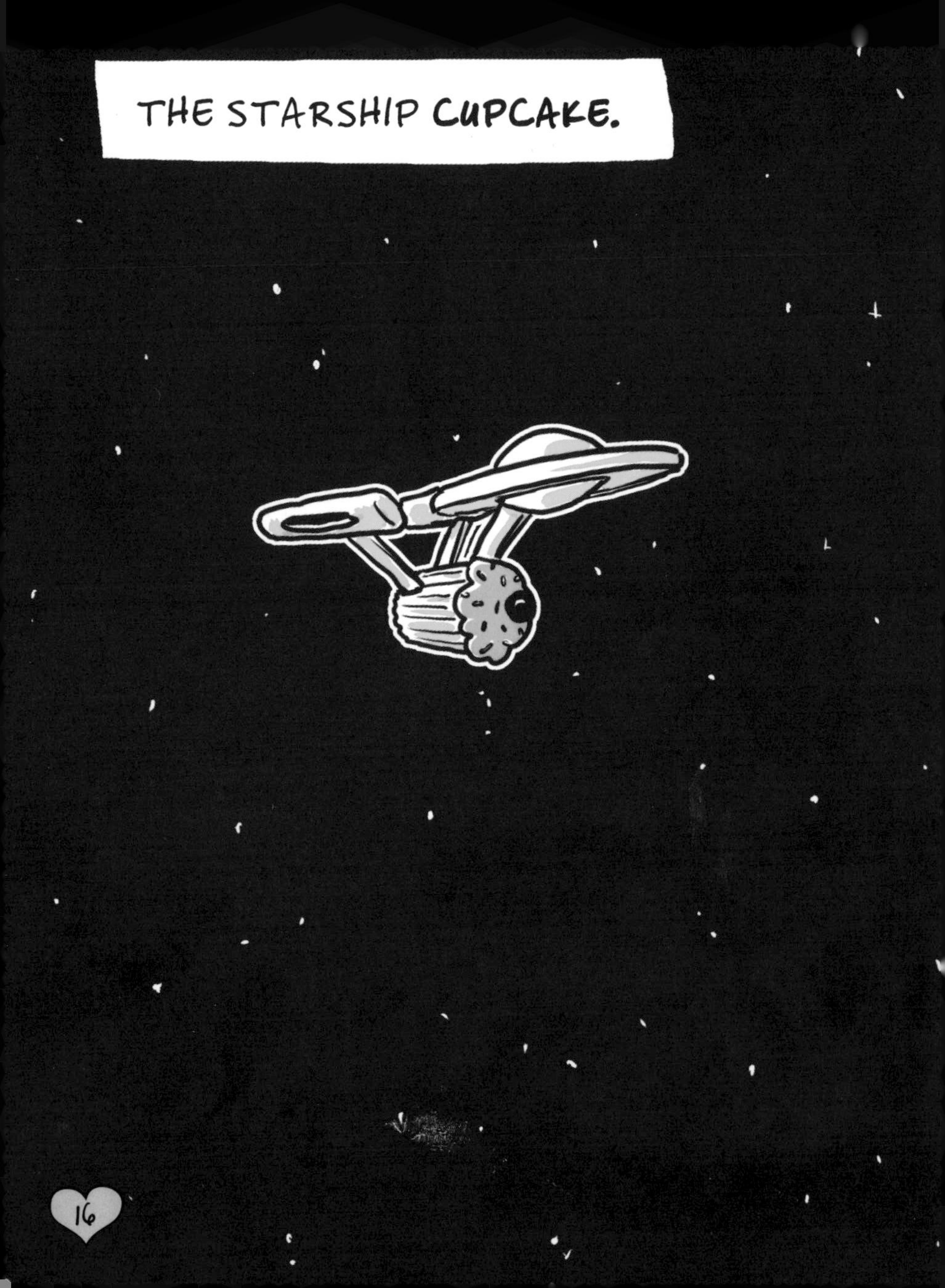
THE STARSHIP CUPCAKE.

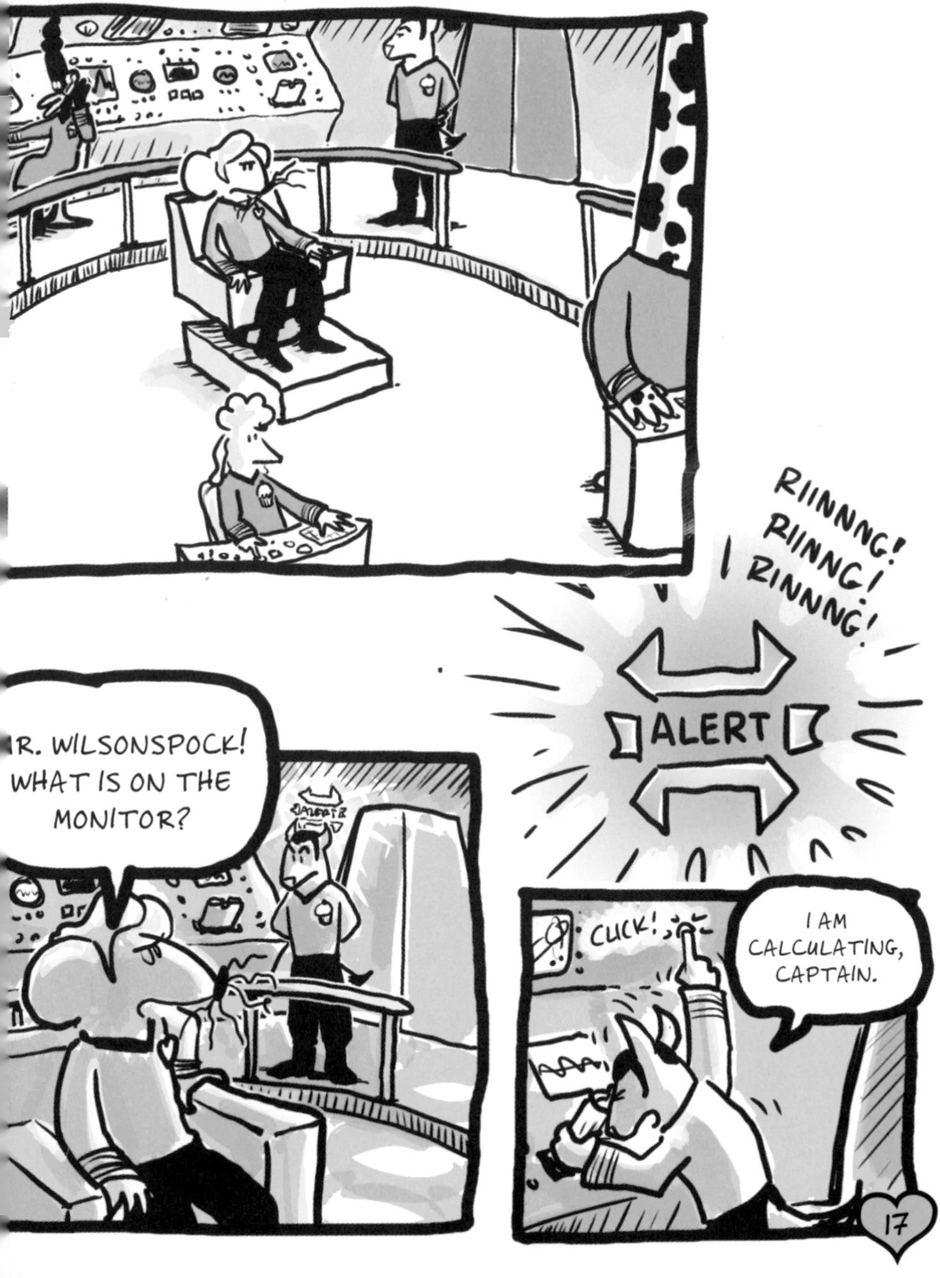
RIINNNG!
RIINNG!
RINNNG!
ALERT
R. WILSONSPOCK! WHAT IS ON THE MONITOR?
CLICK!
I AM CALCULATING, CAPTAIN.

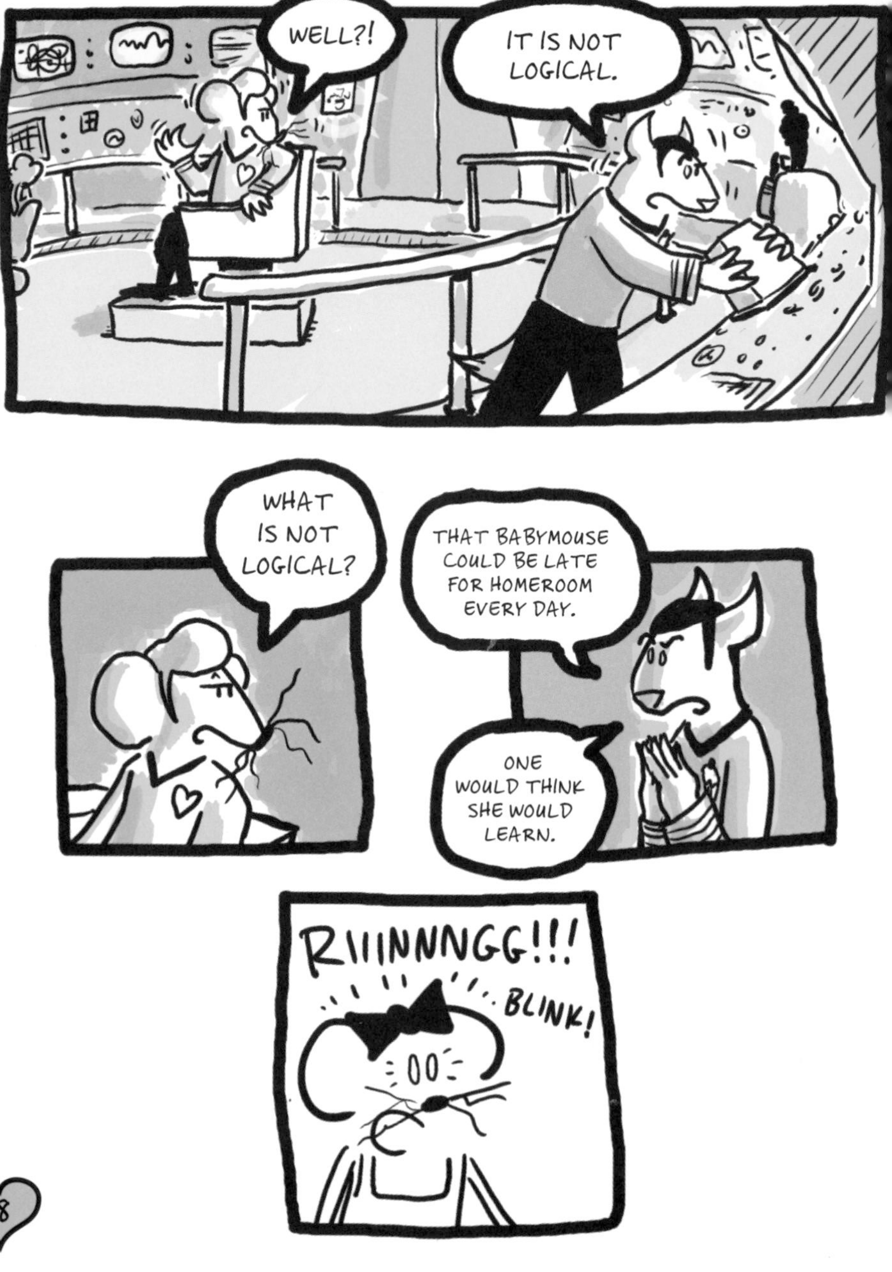
WELL?!
IT IS NOT LOGICAL.
WHAT IS NOT LOGICAL?
THAT BABYMOUSE COULD BE LATE FOR HOMEROOM EVERY DAY.
ONE WOULD THINK SHE WOULD LEARN.
RIIINNNGG!!!
BLINK!

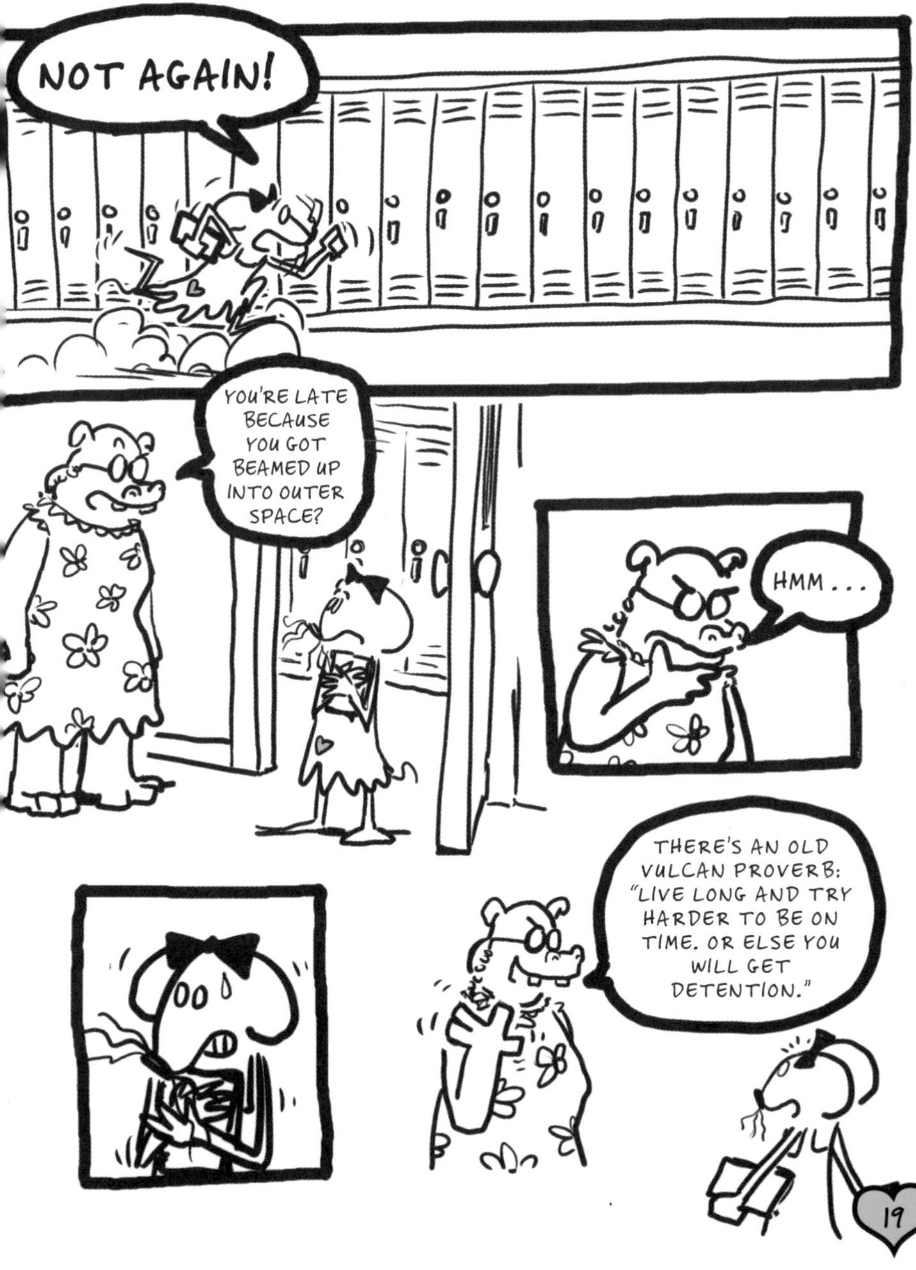
NOT AGAIN!
YOU'RE LATE BECAUSE YOU GOT BEAMED UP INTO OUTER SPACE?
HMM . . .
THERE'S AN OLD VULCAN PROVERB: "LIVE LONG AND TRY HARDER TO BE ON TIME. OR ELSE YOU WILL GET DETENTION."

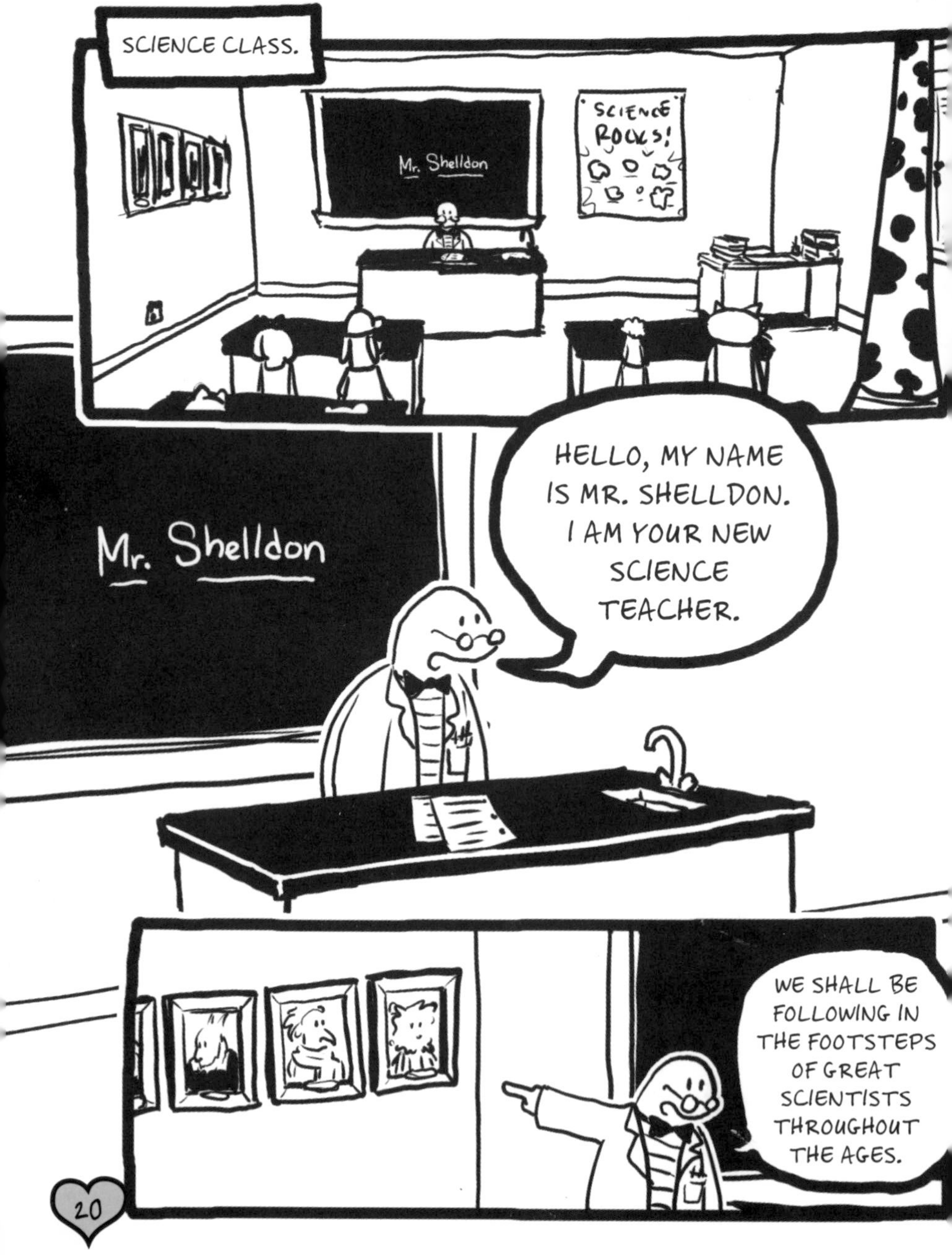
SCIENCE CLASS.
Mr. Shelldon
SCIENCE ROCKS!
Mr. Shelldon
HELLO, MY NAME IS MR. SHELLDON. I AM YOUR NEW SCIENCE TEACHER.
WE SHALL BE FOLLOWING IN THE FOOTSTEPS OF GREAT SCIENTISTS THROUGHOUT THE AGES.

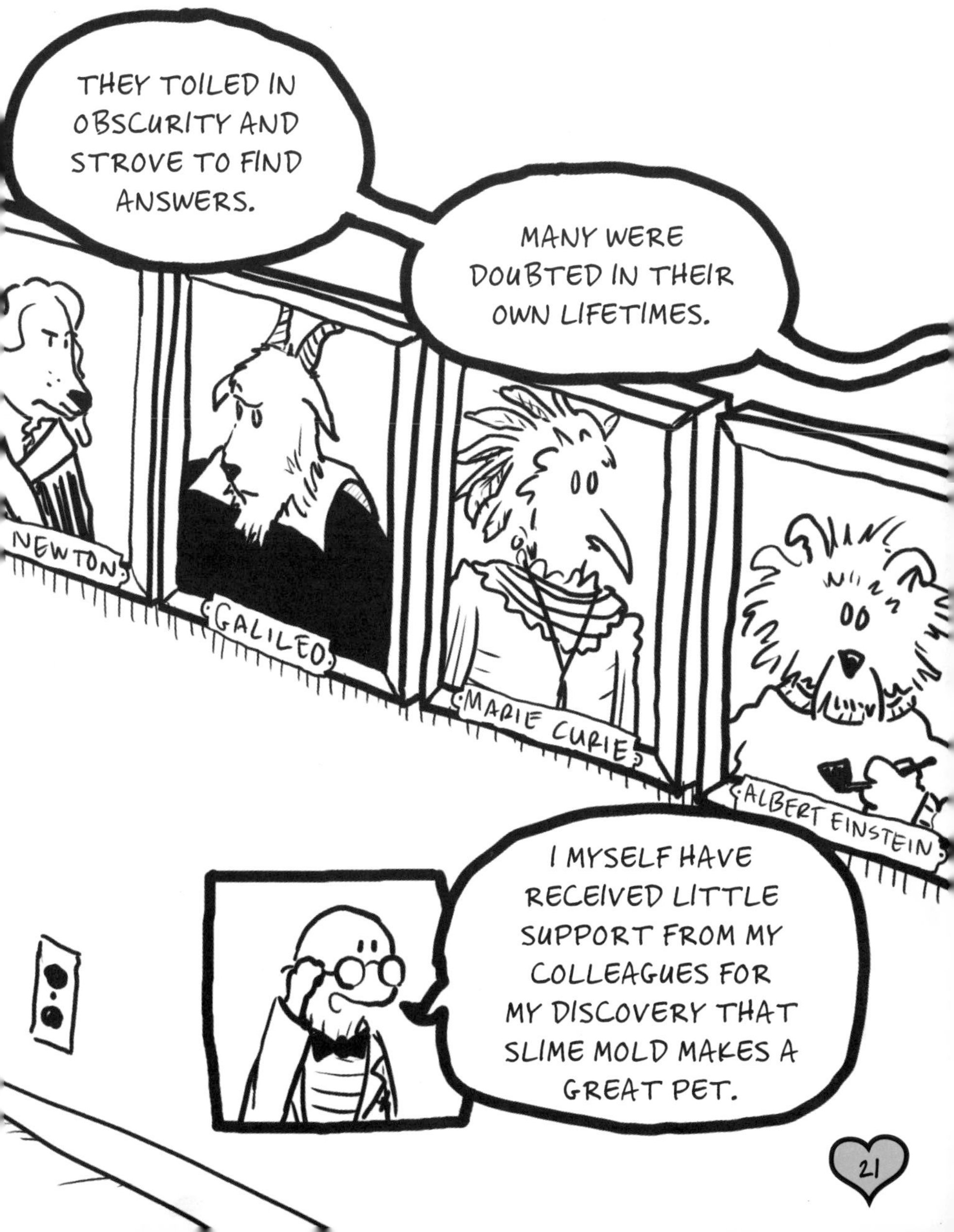
THEY TOILED IN OBSCURITY AND STROVE TO FIND ANSWERS.
MANY WERE DOUBTED IN THEIR OWN LIFETIMES.
NEWTON
GALILEO
MARIE CURIE
ALBERT EINSTEIN
I MYSELF HAVE RECEIVED LITTLE SUPPORT FROM MY COLLEAGUES FOR MY DISCOVERY THAT SLIME MOLD MAKES A GREAT PET.

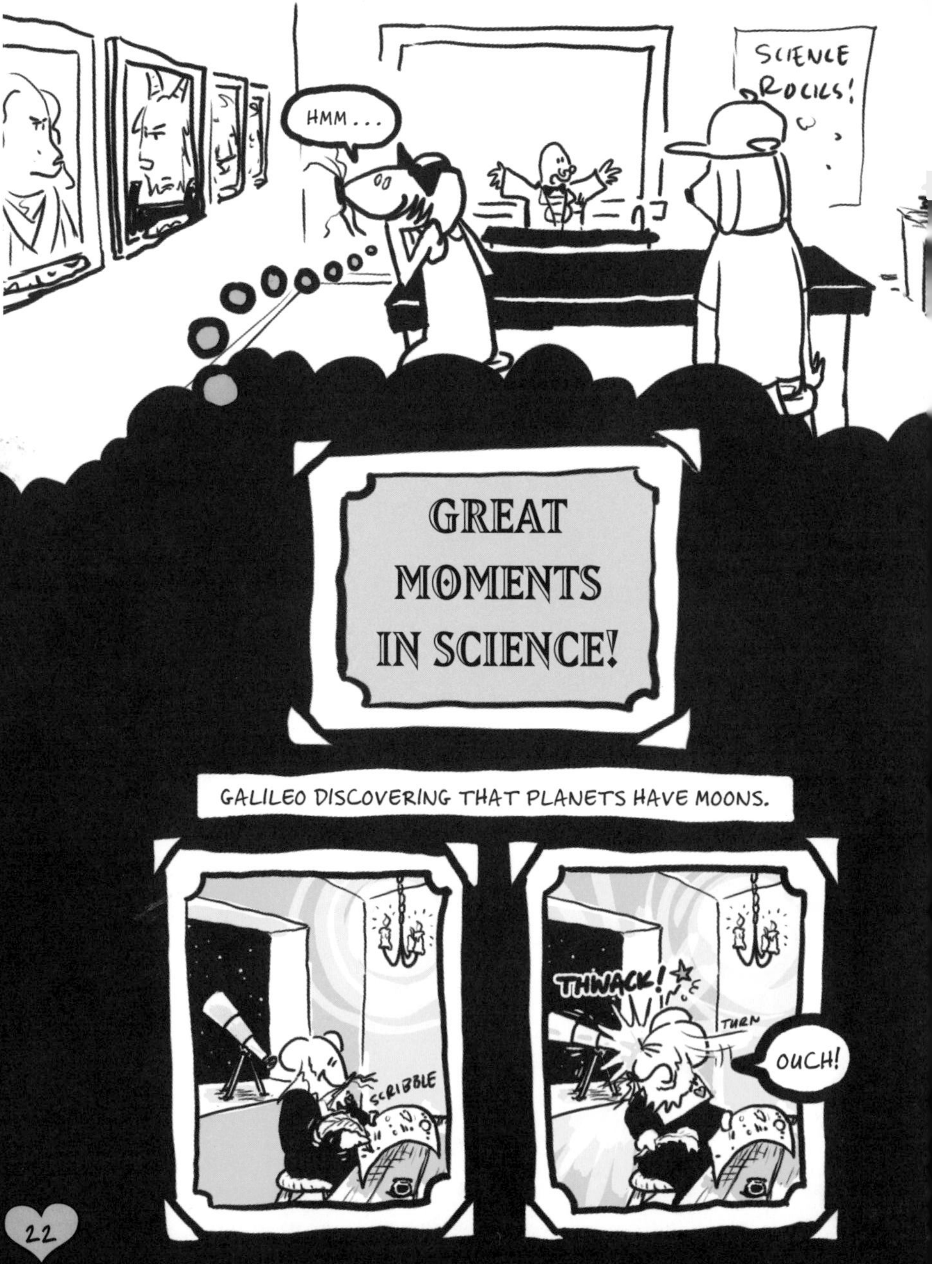
SCIENCE ROCKS!
HMM...
GREAT MOMENTS IN SCIENCE!
GALILEO DISCOVERING THAT PLANETS HAVE MOONS.
SCRIBBLE
THWACK!
TURN
OUCH!

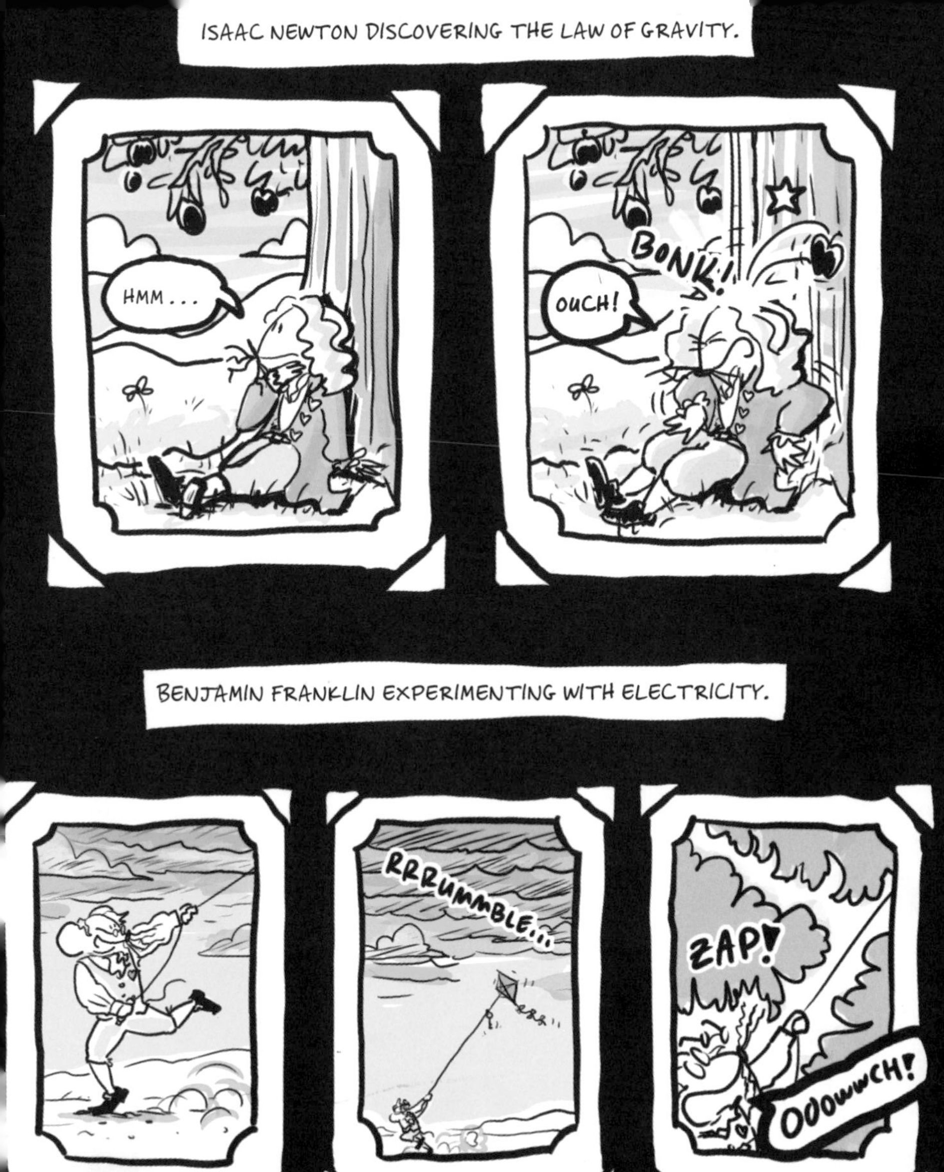
ISAAC NEWTON DISCOVERING THE LAW OF GRAVITY.
HMM...
BONK!
OUCH!
BENJAMIN FRANKLIN EXPERIMENTING WITH ELECTRICITY.
RRRUMMBLE...
ZAP!
OOOWWCH!

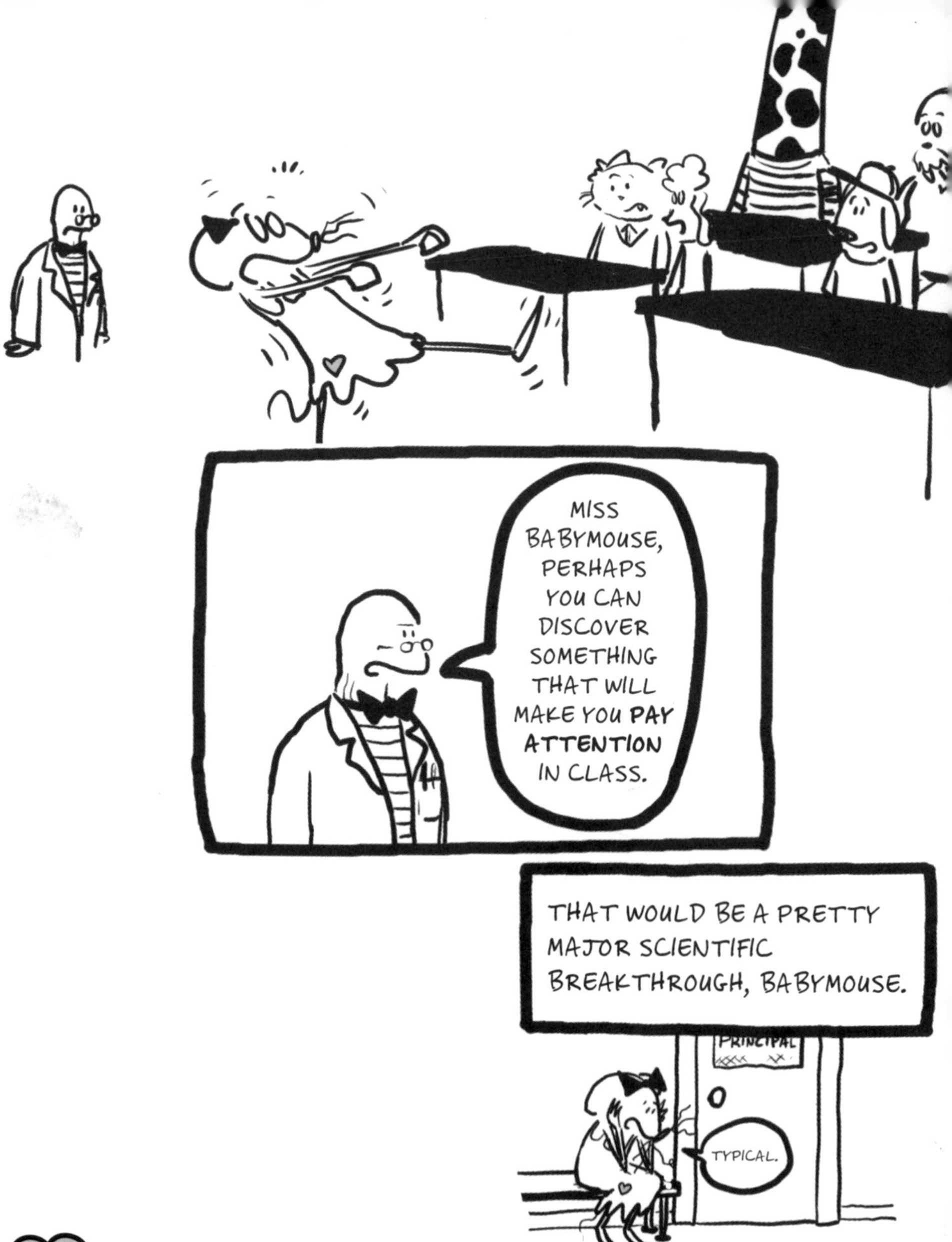

MISS BABYMOUSE, PERHAPS YOU CAN DISCOVER SOMETHING THAT WILL MAKE YOU **PAY ATTENTION** IN CLASS.
THAT WOULD BE A PRETTY MAJOR SCIENTIFIC BREAKTHROUGH, BABYMOUSE.
PRINCIPAL
TYPICAL.

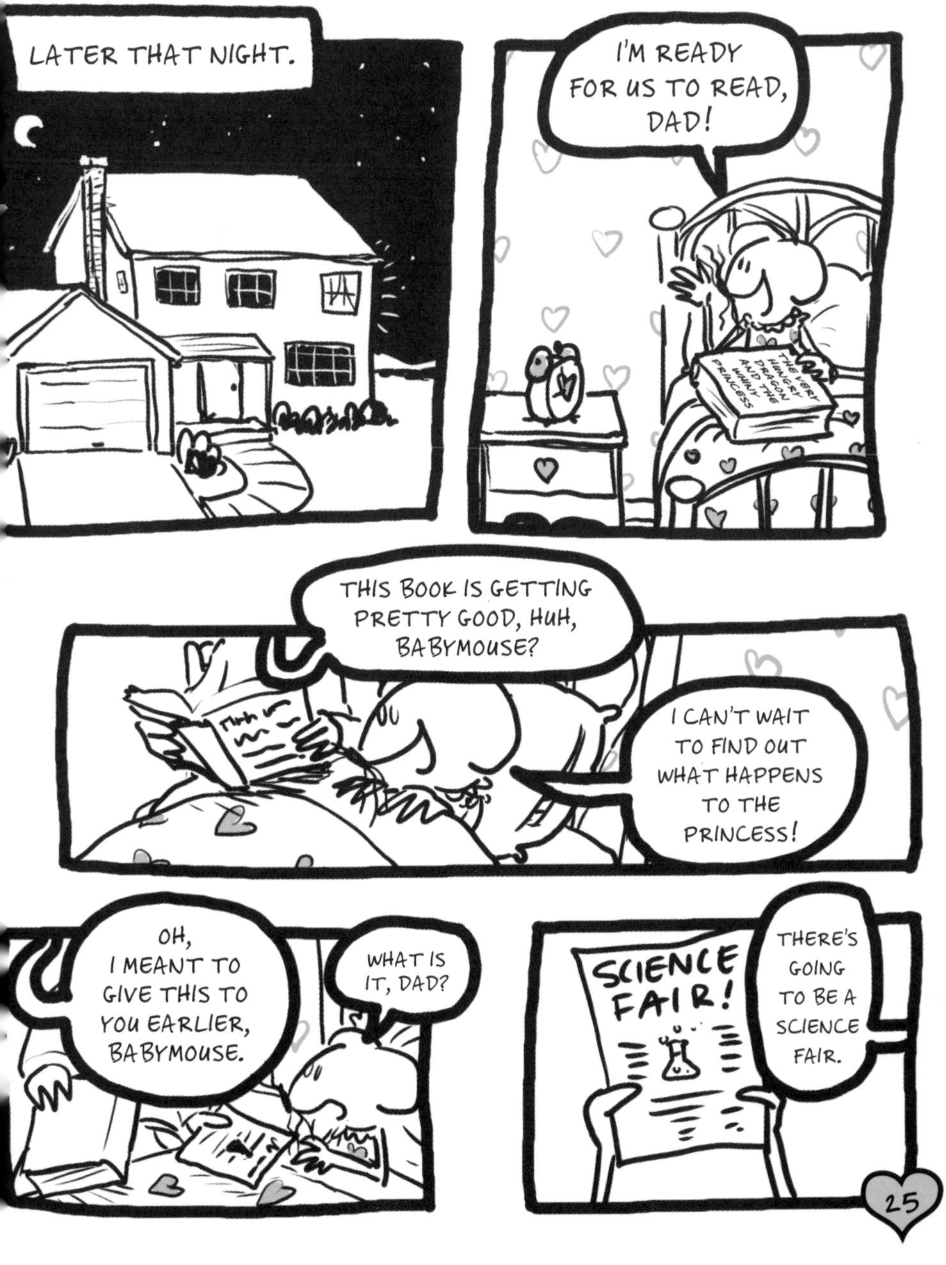
LATER THAT NIGHT.
I'M READY FOR US TO READ, DAD!
THE VERY HUNGRY DRAGON AND THE WHINY PRINCESS
THIS BOOK IS GETTING PRETTY GOOD, HUH, BABYMOUSE?
I CAN'T WAIT TO FIND OUT WHAT HAPPENS TO THE PRINCESS!
OH, I MEANT TO GIVE THIS TO YOU EARLIER, BABYMOUSE.
WHAT IS IT, DAD?
SCIENCE FAIR!
THERE'S GOING TO BE A SCIENCE FAIR.

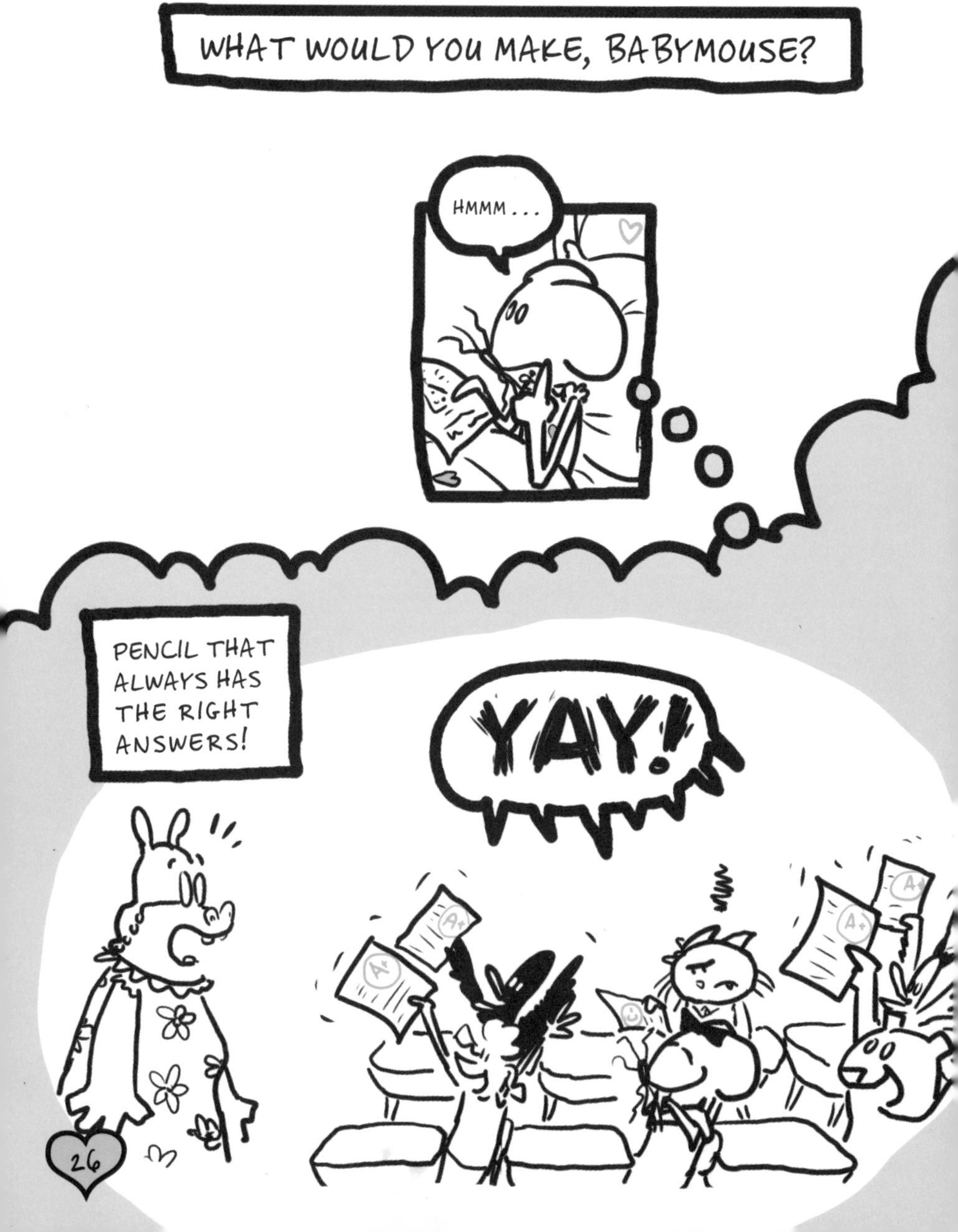
WHAT WOULD YOU MAKE, BABYMOUSE?
HMMM...
PENCIL THAT ALWAYS HAS THE RIGHT ANSWERS!
YAY!
A+
A+
A+
A+
A+
26

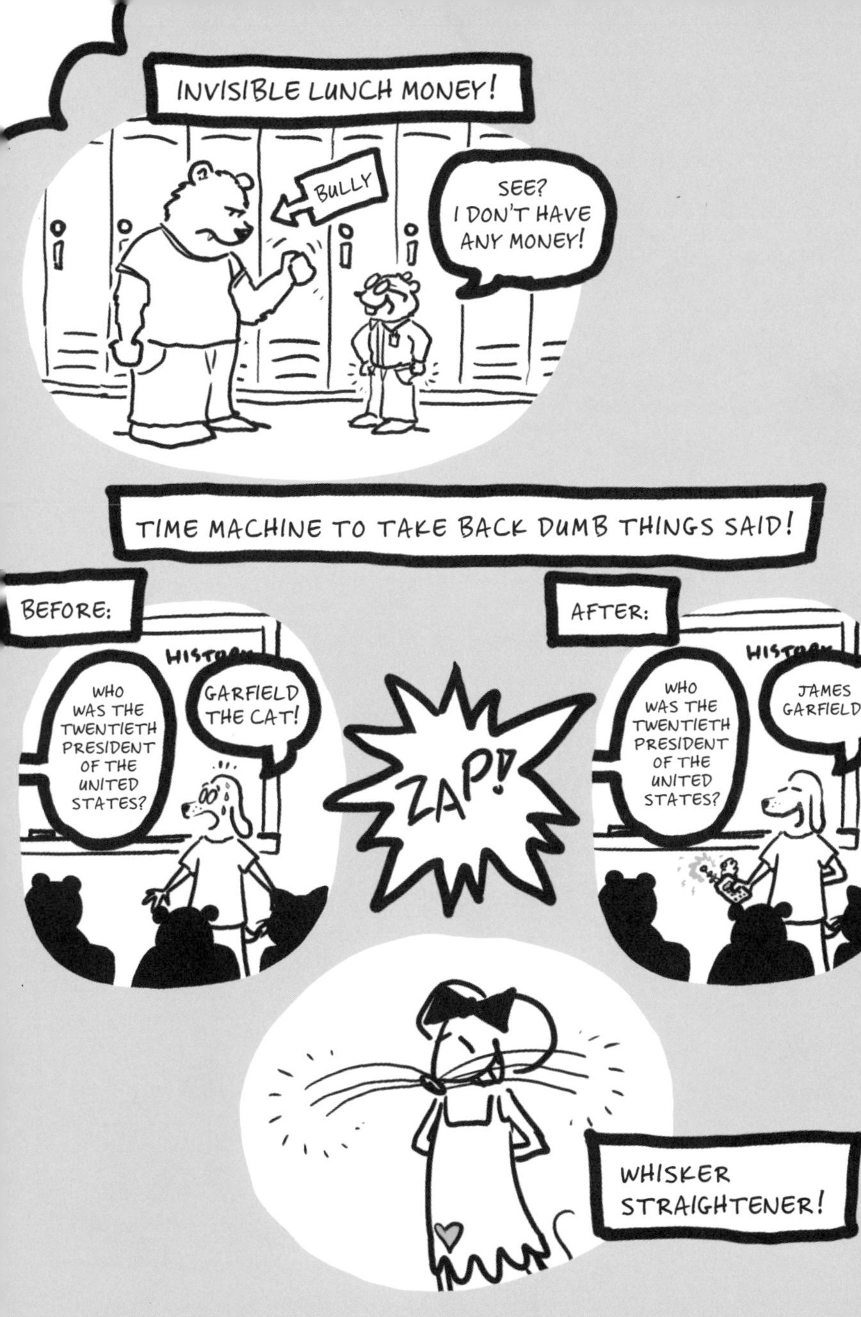
INVISIBLE LUNCH MONEY!
BULLY
SEE? I DON'T HAVE ANY MONEY!
TIME MACHINE TO TAKE BACK DUMB THINGS SAID!
BEFORE:
HISTORY
WHO WAS THE TWENTIETH PRESIDENT OF THE UNITED STATES?
GARFIELD THE CAT!
ZAP!
AFTER:
HISTORY
WHO WAS THE TWENTIETH PRESIDENT OF THE UNITED STATES?
JAMES GARFIELD!
WHISKER STRAIGHTENER!

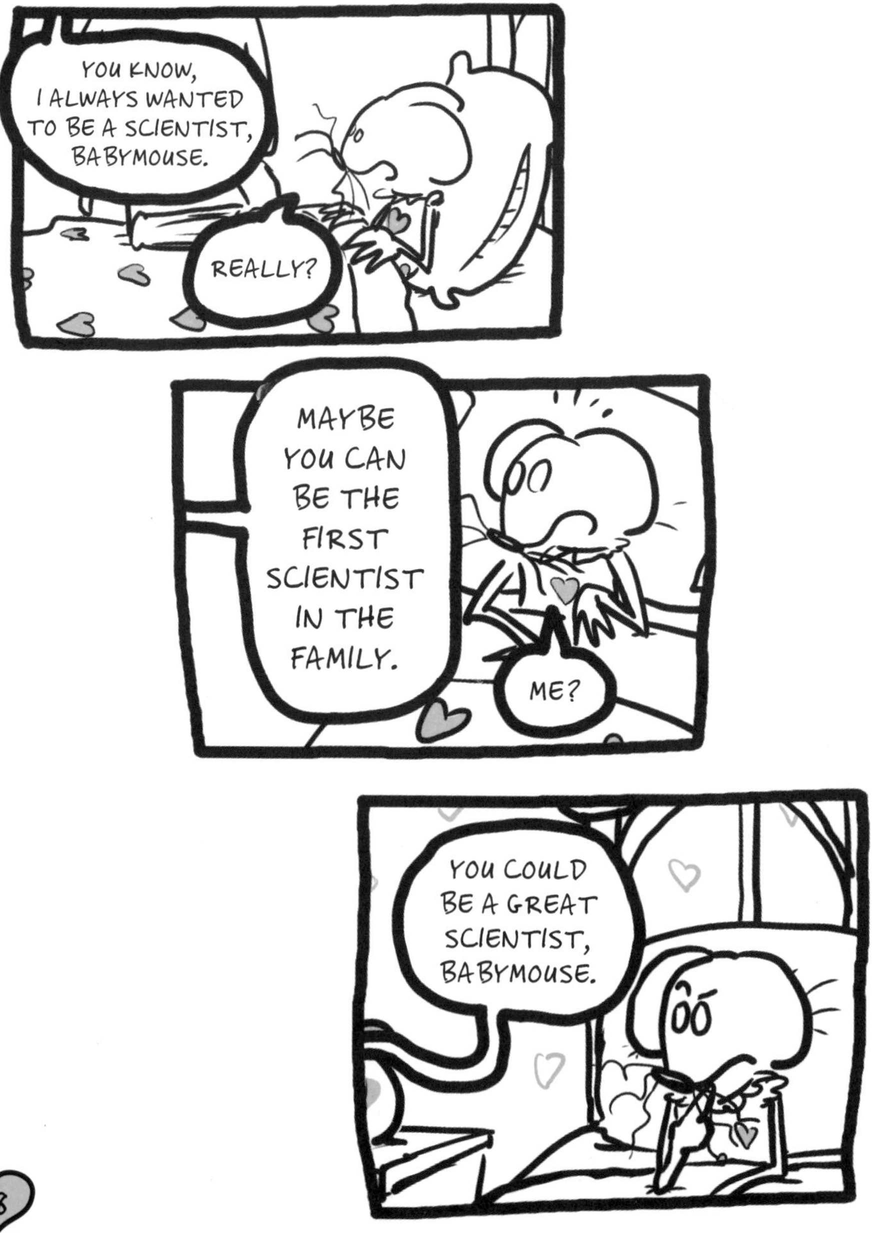
YOU KNOW, I ALWAYS WANTED TO BE A SCIENTIST, BABYMOUSE.
REALLY?
MAYBE YOU CAN BE THE FIRST SCIENTIST IN THE FAMILY.
ME?
YOU COULD BE A GREAT SCIENTIST, BABYMOUSE.

GREAT DISCOVERIES OF DR. BABYMOUSE!

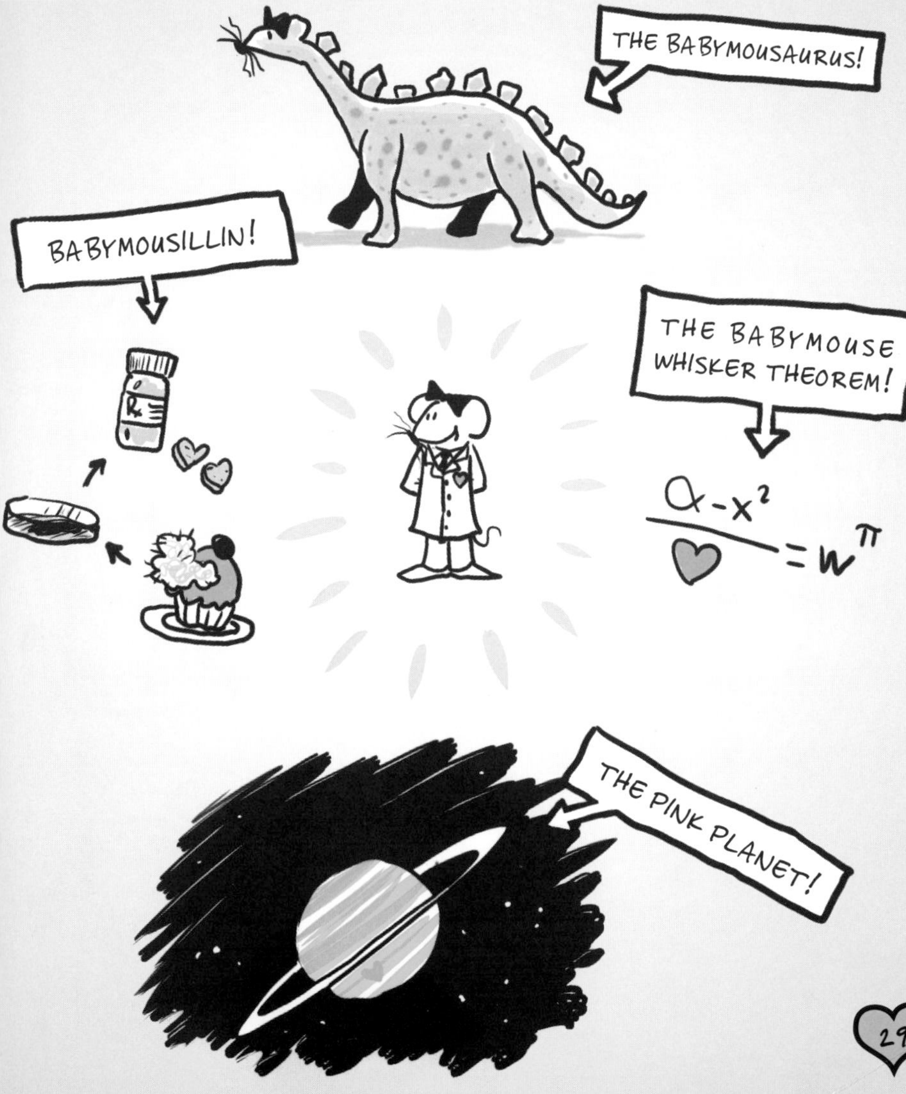
THE BABYMOUSAURUS!
BABYMOUSILLIN!
THE BABYMOUSE WHISKER THEOREM!
α-x²
=w^π
THE PINK PLANET!

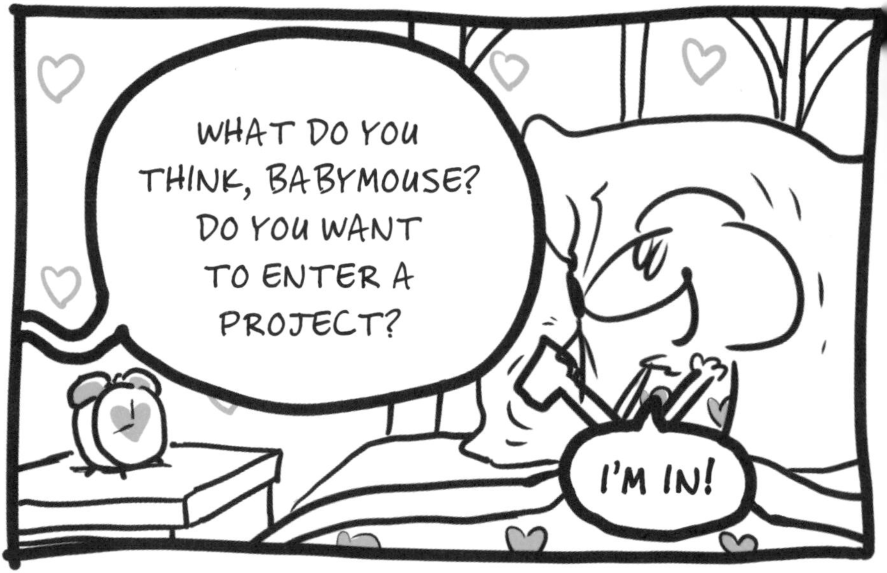
WHAT DO YOU THINK, BABYMOUSE? DO YOU WANT TO ENTER A PROJECT?
I'M IN!

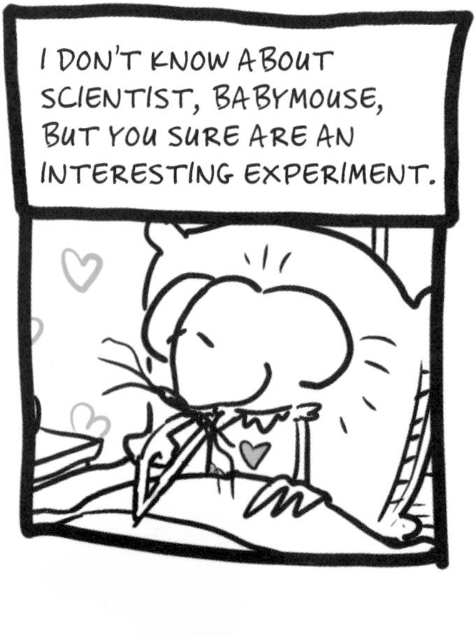
I DON'T KNOW ABOUT SCIENTIST, BABYMOUSE, BUT YOU SURE ARE AN INTERESTING EXPERIMENT.

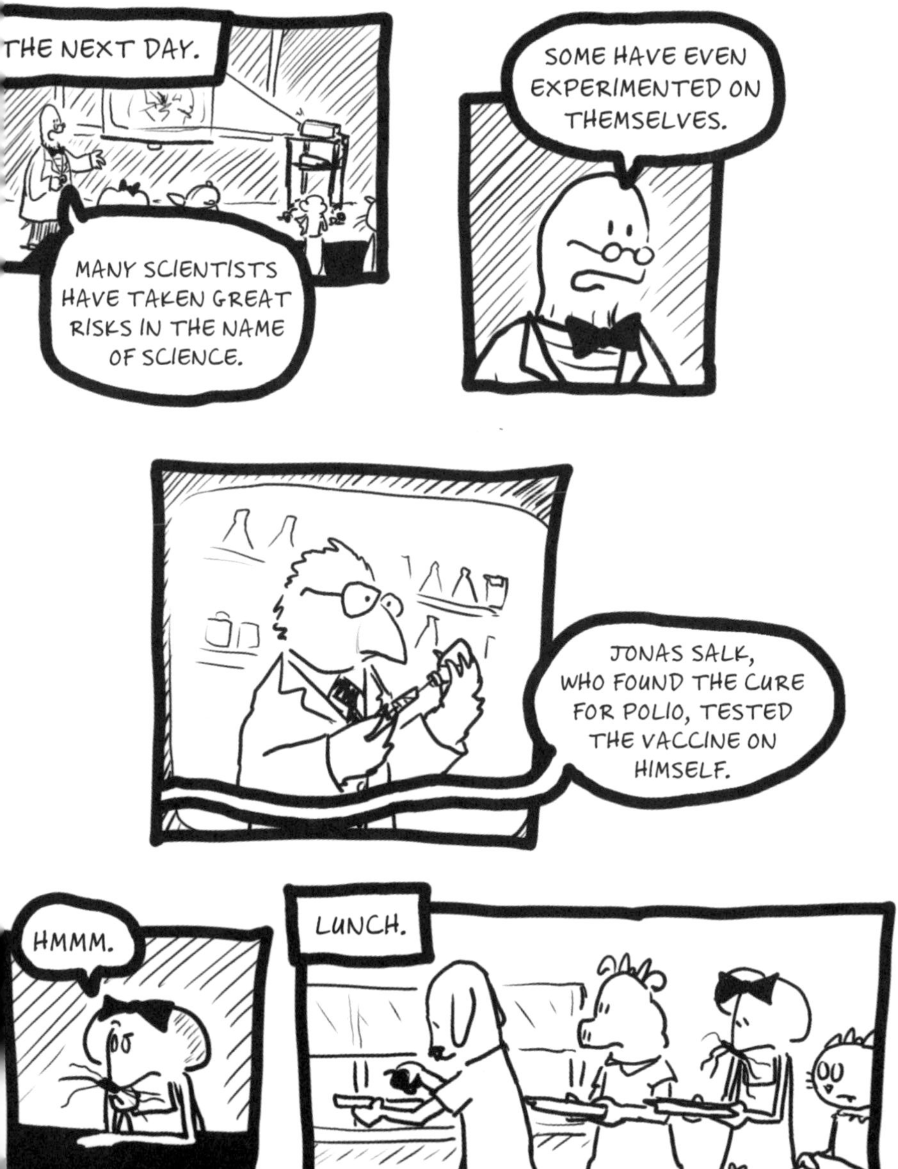
THE NEXT DAY.
MANY SCIENTISTS HAVE TAKEN GREAT RISKS IN THE NAME OF SCIENCE.
SOME HAVE EVEN EXPERIMENTED ON THEMSELVES.
JONAS SALK, WHO FOUND THE CURE FOR POLIO, TESTED THE VACCINE ON HIMSELF.
HMMM.
LUNCH.

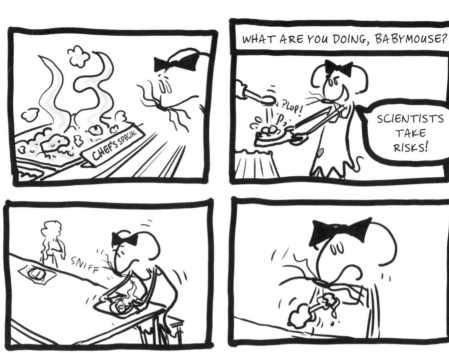

WHAT ARE YOU DOING, BABYMOUSE?

PLOP!

SCIENTISTS TAKE RISKS!

CHEF'S SPECIAL

SNIFF

BITE!

CHEW

ACK!

YOU KNOW, BABYMOUSE, IT DIDN'T END SO WELL FOR MARIE CURIE, EITHER.

UGH.

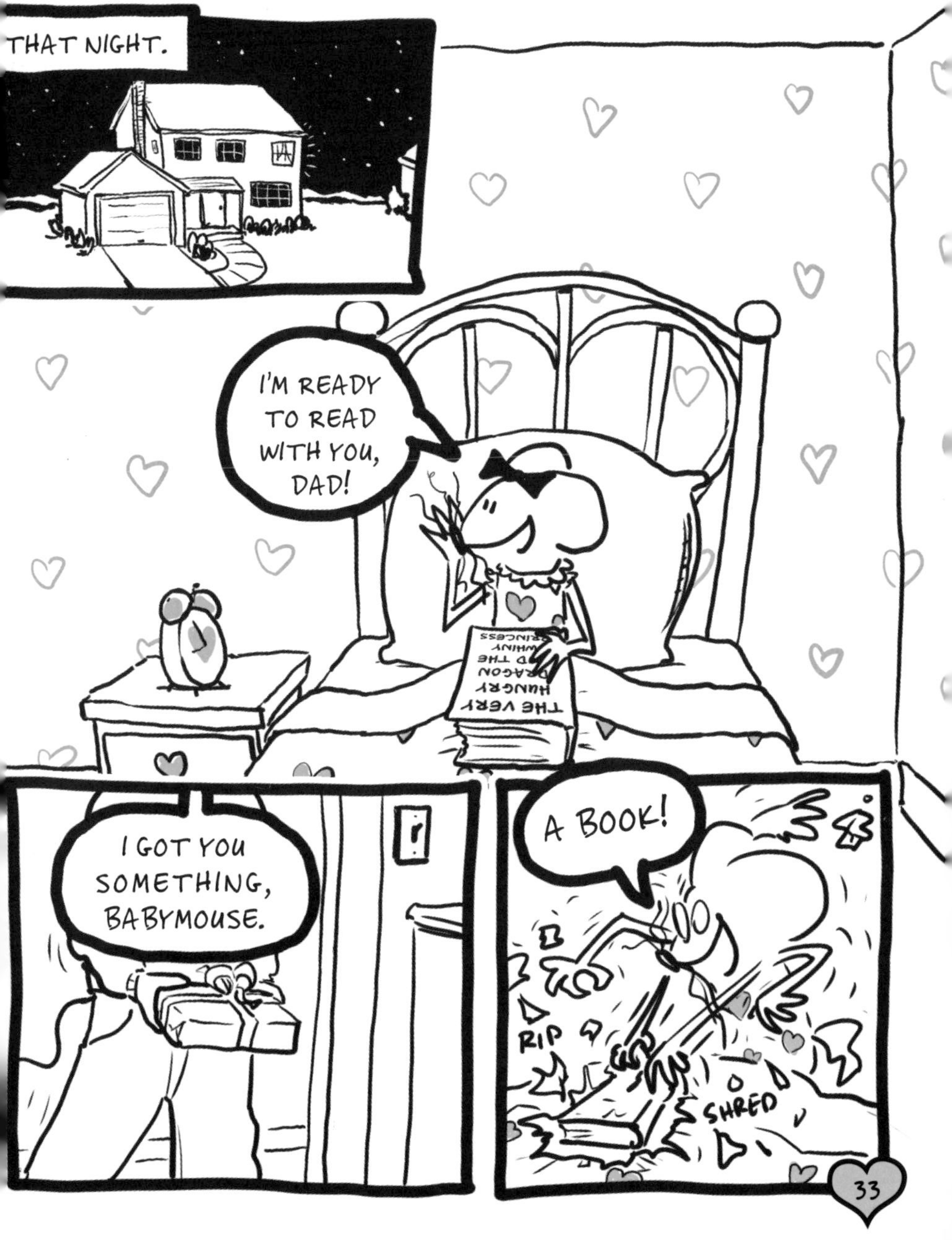
THAT NIGHT.
I'M READY TO READ WITH YOU, DAD!
THE VERY HUNGRY DRAGON AND THE WHINY PRINCESS
I GOT YOU SOMETHING, BABYMOUSE.
A BOOK!
RIP
SHRED

I THOUGHT IT WOULD BE INSPIRING FOR YOUR SCIENCE FAIR PROJECT, BABYMOUSE.

OH...

OOH, LOOK! THERE'S A PARTICLE ACCELERATOR AND A BAKING-SODA VOLCANO AND, OOH— WOW!—AMOEBAS!

AND A BLAH, AND HERE'S A BLAH BLAH BLAH...

101 EASY-PEASY SCIENCE FAIR PROJECTS

THE VERY HUNGRY DRAGON AND THE WHINY PRINCESS

WHERE'S YOUR SENSE OF SCIENTIFIC CURIOSITY, BABYMOUSE?

BUT I AM CURIOUS! I WANT TO KNOW IF THAT DRAGON EATS THE PRINCESS!

-PEASY SCIENCE

HUNGRY DRAGON AND THE WHINY PRINCESS

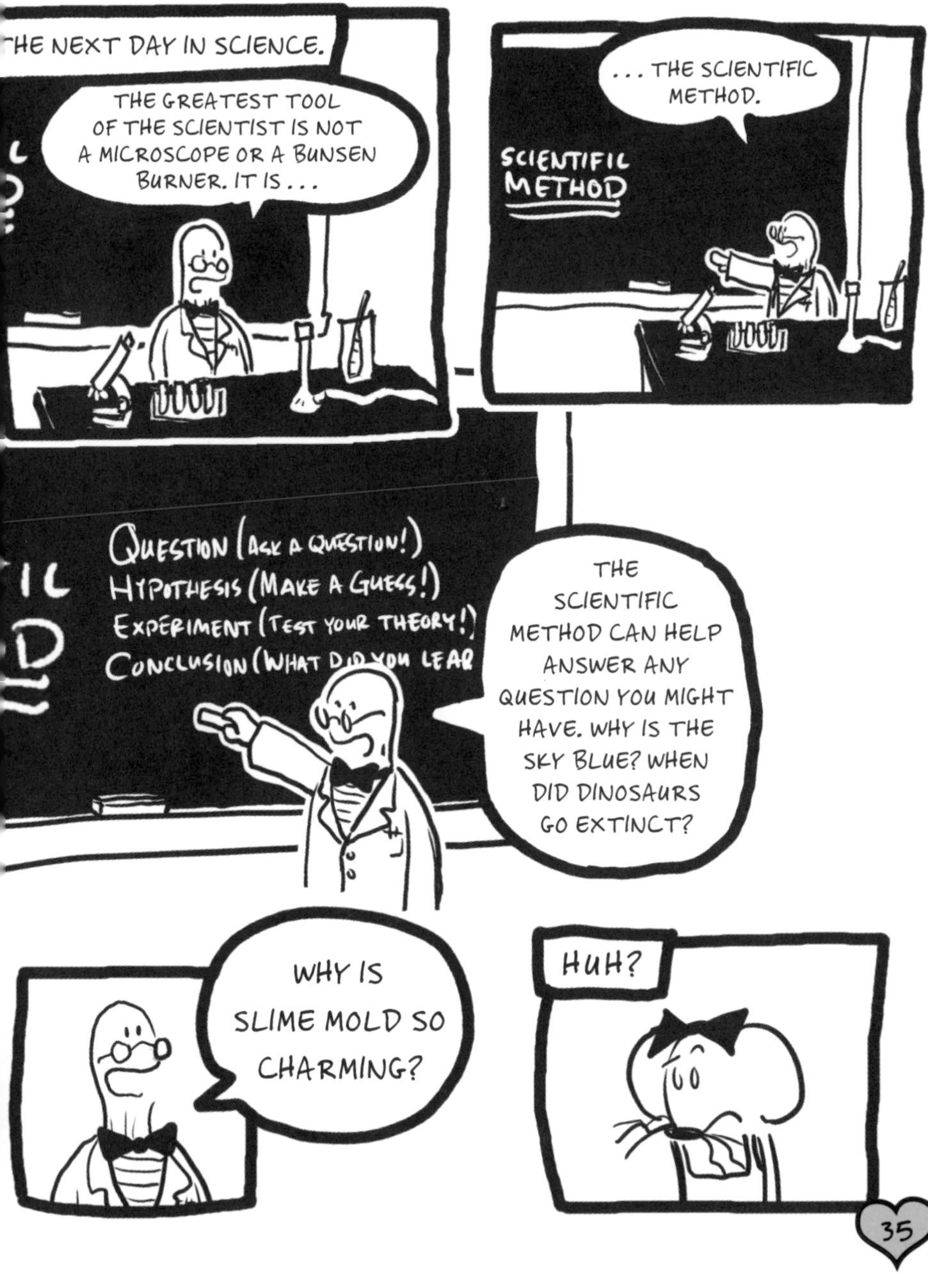

THE NEXT DAY IN SCIENCE.
THE GREATEST TOOL OF THE SCIENTIST IS NOT A MICROSCOPE OR A BUNSEN BURNER. IT IS . . .
. . . THE SCIENTIFIC METHOD.
SCIENTIFIC METHOD
QUESTION (ASK A QUESTION!)
HYPOTHESIS (MAKE A GUESS!)
EXPERIMENT (TEST YOUR THEORY!)
CONCLUSION (WHAT DID YOU LEAR
THE SCIENTIFIC METHOD CAN HELP ANSWER ANY QUESTION YOU MIGHT HAVE. WHY IS THE SKY BLUE? WHEN DID DINOSAURS GO EXTINCT?
WHY IS SLIME MOLD SO CHARMING?
HUH?

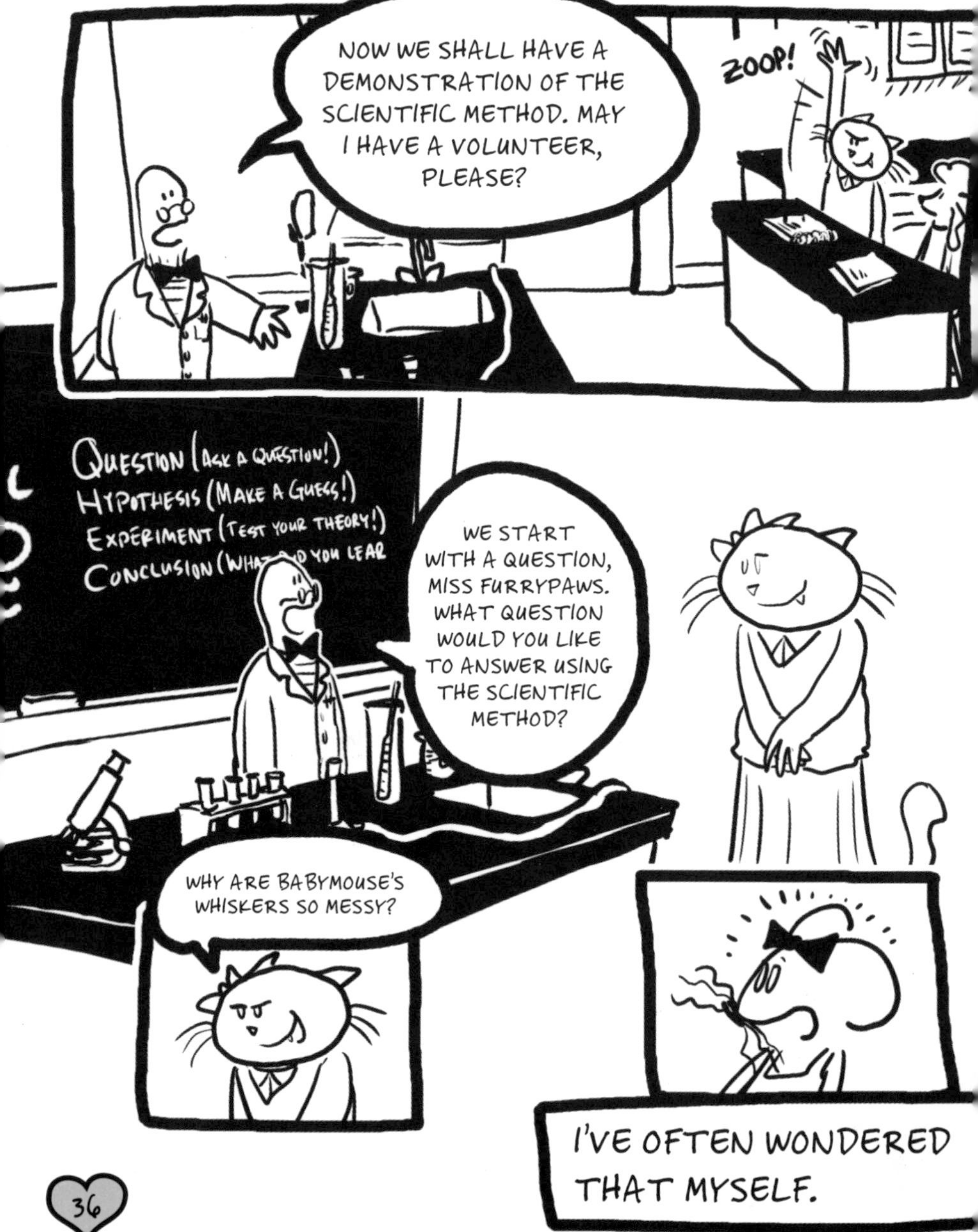
NOW WE SHALL HAVE A DEMONSTRATION OF THE SCIENTIFIC METHOD. MAY I HAVE A VOLUNTEER, PLEASE?
ZOOP!
QUESTION (ASK A QUESTION!)
HYPOTHESIS (MAKE A GUESS!)
EXPERIMENT (TEST YOUR THEORY!)
CONCLUSION (WHA
D YOU LEAR
WE START WITH A QUESTION, MISS FURRYPAWS. WHAT QUESTION WOULD YOU LIKE TO ANSWER USING THE SCIENTIFIC METHOD?
WHY ARE BABYMOUSE'S WHISKERS SO MESSY?
I'VE OFTEN WONDERED THAT MYSELF.

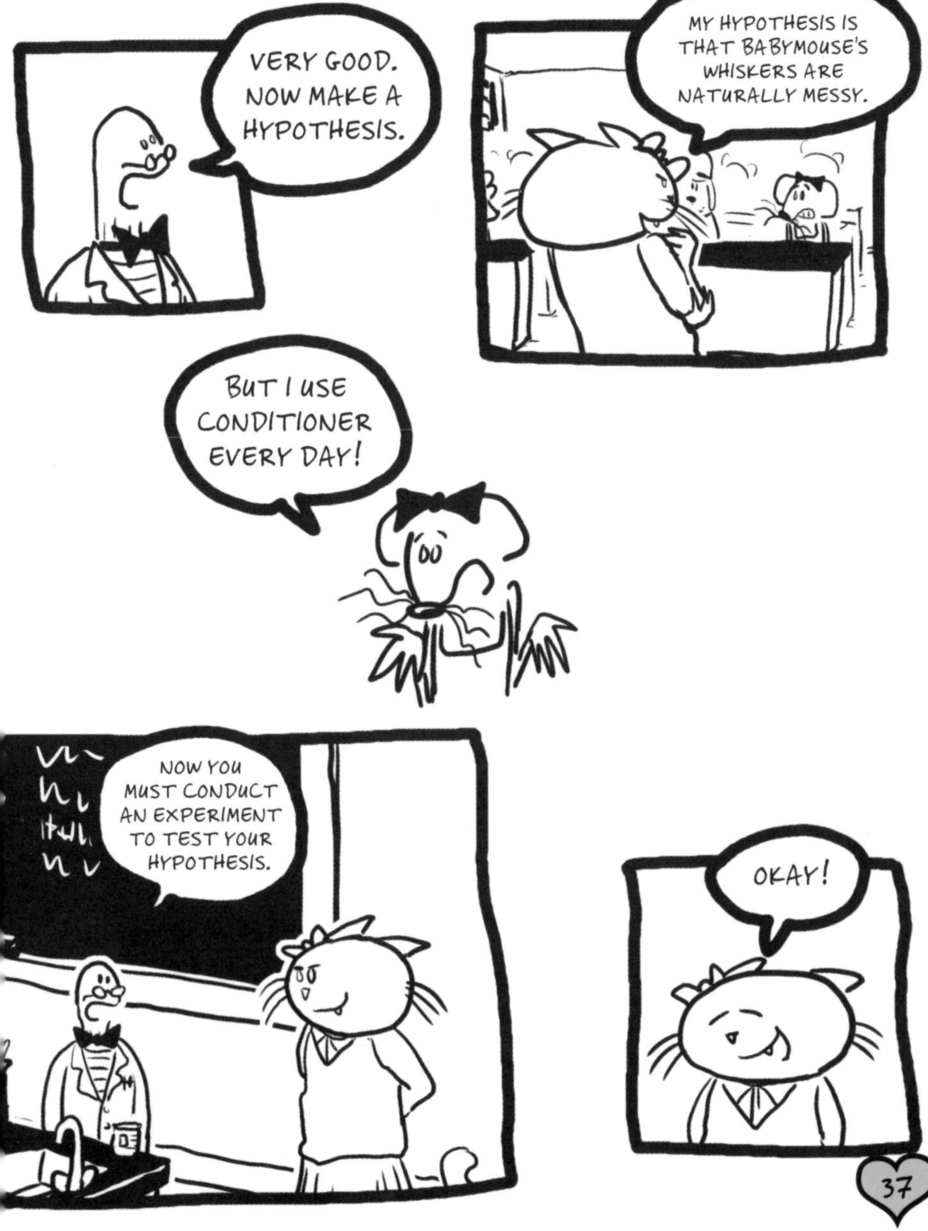

VERY GOOD. NOW MAKE A HYPOTHESIS.
MY HYPOTHESIS IS THAT BABYMOUSE'S WHISKERS ARE NATURALLY MESSY.
BUT I USE CONDITIONER EVERY DAY!
NOW YOU MUST CONDUCT AN EXPERIMENT TO TEST YOUR HYPOTHESIS.
OKAY!

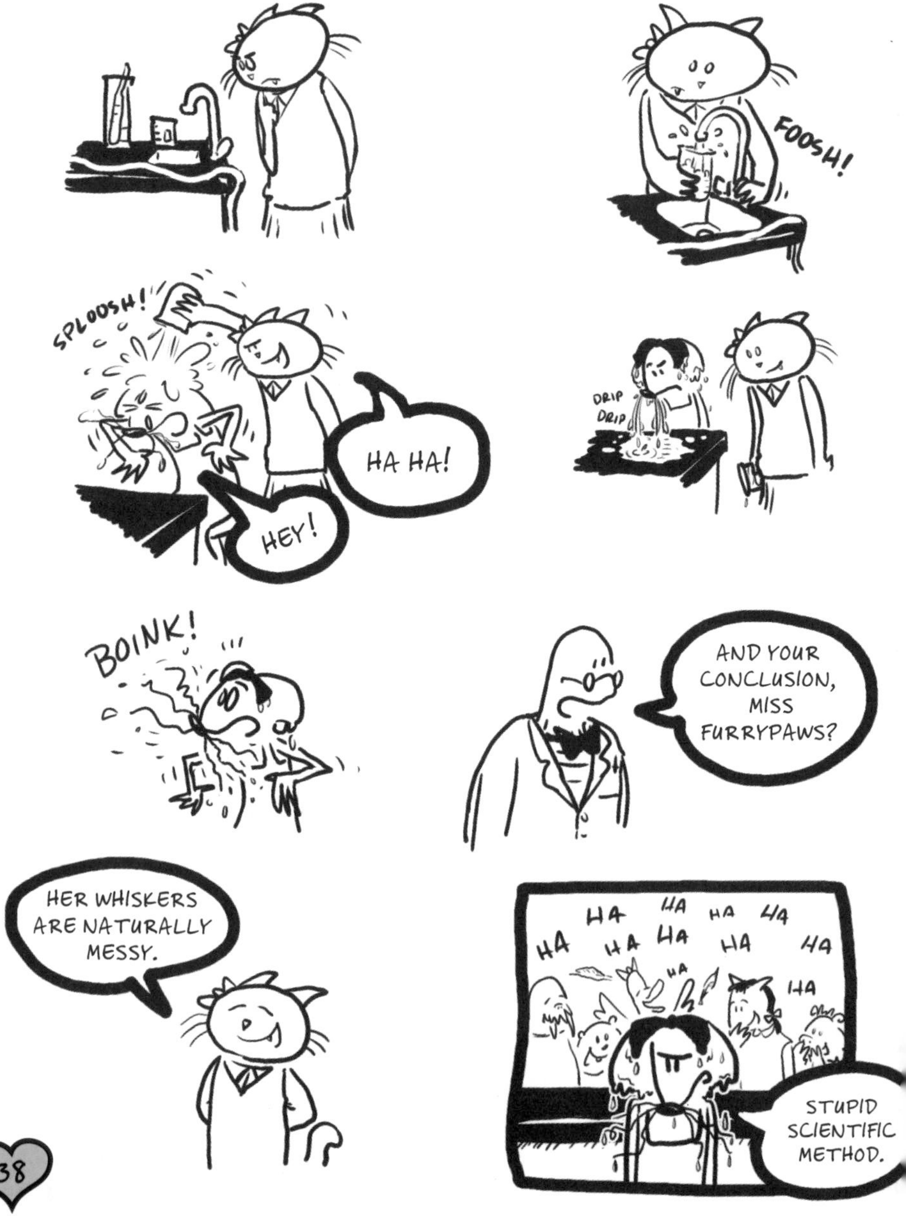
FOOSH!
SPLOOSH!
HA HA!
HEY!
DRIP
DRIP
BOINK!
AND YOUR CONCLUSION, MISS FURRYPAWS?
HER WHISKERS ARE NATURALLY MESSY.
HA HA HA HA HA HA HA HA HA HA HA HA
STUPID SCIENTIFIC METHOD.

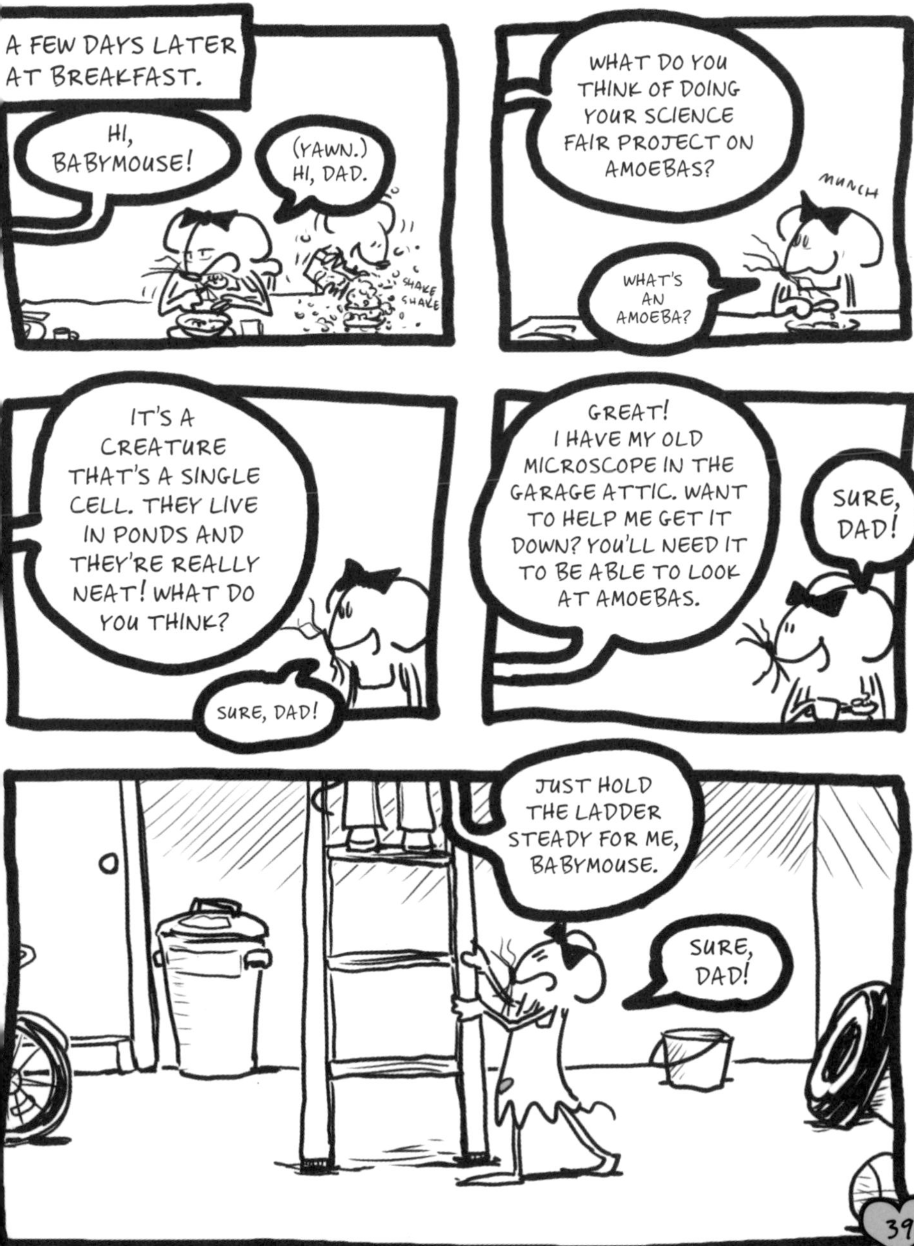
A FEW DAYS LATER AT BREAKFAST.
HI, BABYMOUSE!
(YAWN.) HI, DAD.
SHAKE SHAKE
WHAT DO YOU THINK OF DOING YOUR SCIENCE FAIR PROJECT ON AMOEBAS?
MUNCH
WHAT'S AN AMOEBA?
IT'S A CREATURE THAT'S A SINGLE CELL. THEY LIVE IN PONDS AND THEY'RE REALLY NEAT! WHAT DO YOU THINK?
SURE, DAD!
GREAT! I HAVE MY OLD MICROSCOPE IN THE GARAGE ATTIC. WANT TO HELP ME GET IT DOWN? YOU'LL NEED IT TO BE ABLE TO LOOK AT AMOEBAS.
SURE, DAD!
JUST HOLD THE LADDER STEADY FOR ME, BABYMOUSE.
SURE, DAD!

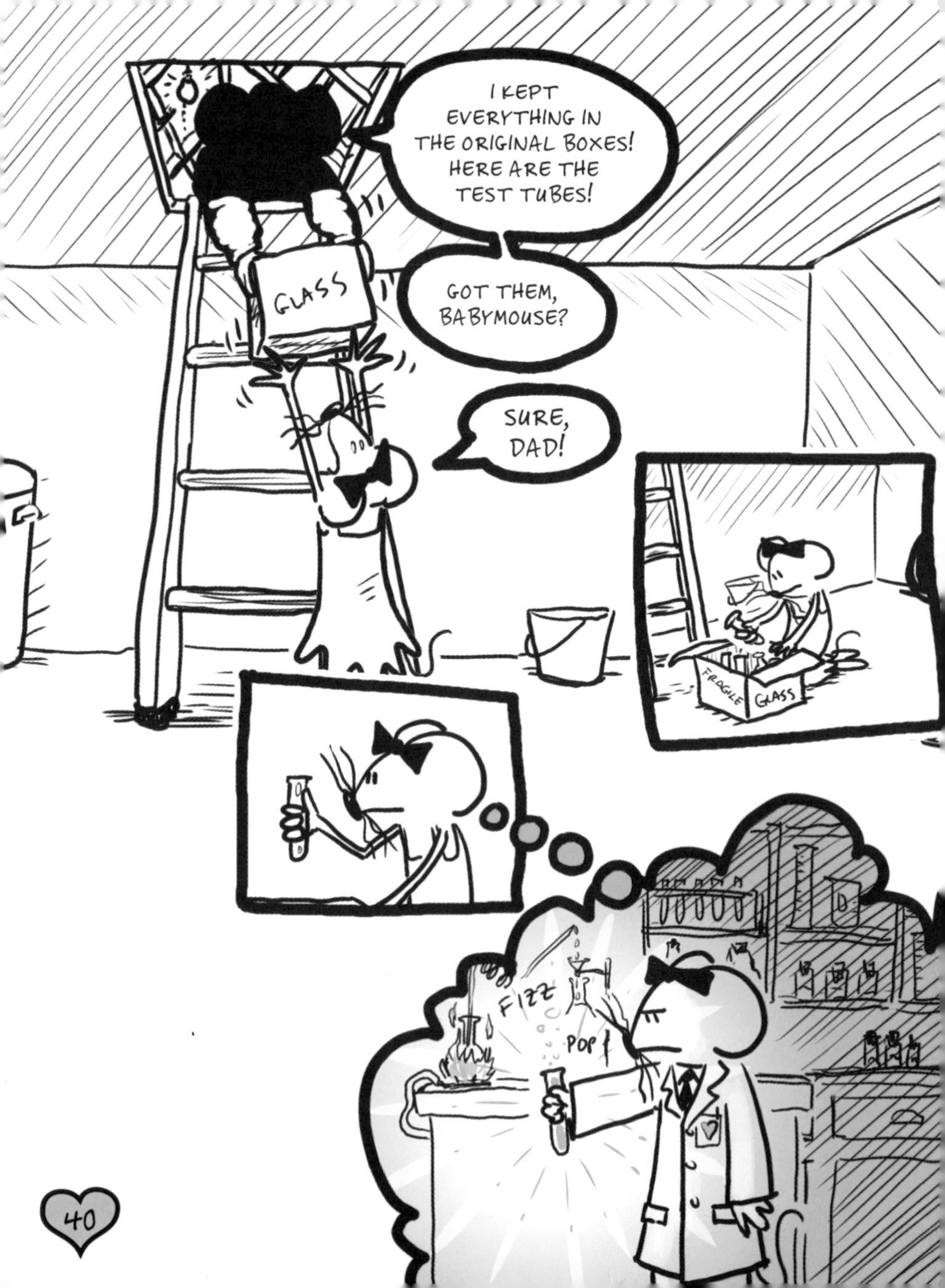
I KEPT EVERYTHING IN THE ORIGINAL BOXES! HERE ARE THE TEST TUBES!
GLASS
GOT THEM, BABYMOUSE?
SURE, DAD!
FRAGILE
GLASS
FIZZ
POP

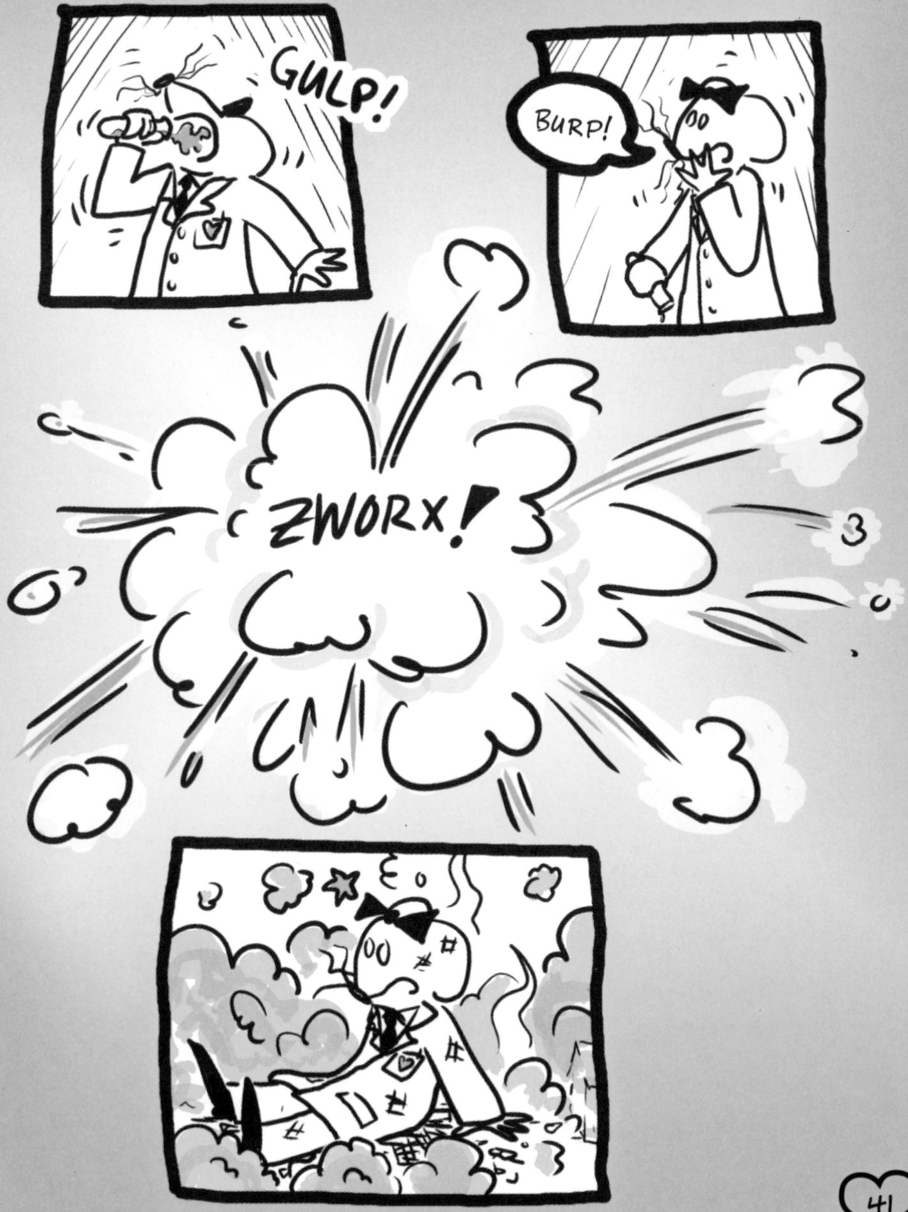
GULP!
BURP!
ZWORX!

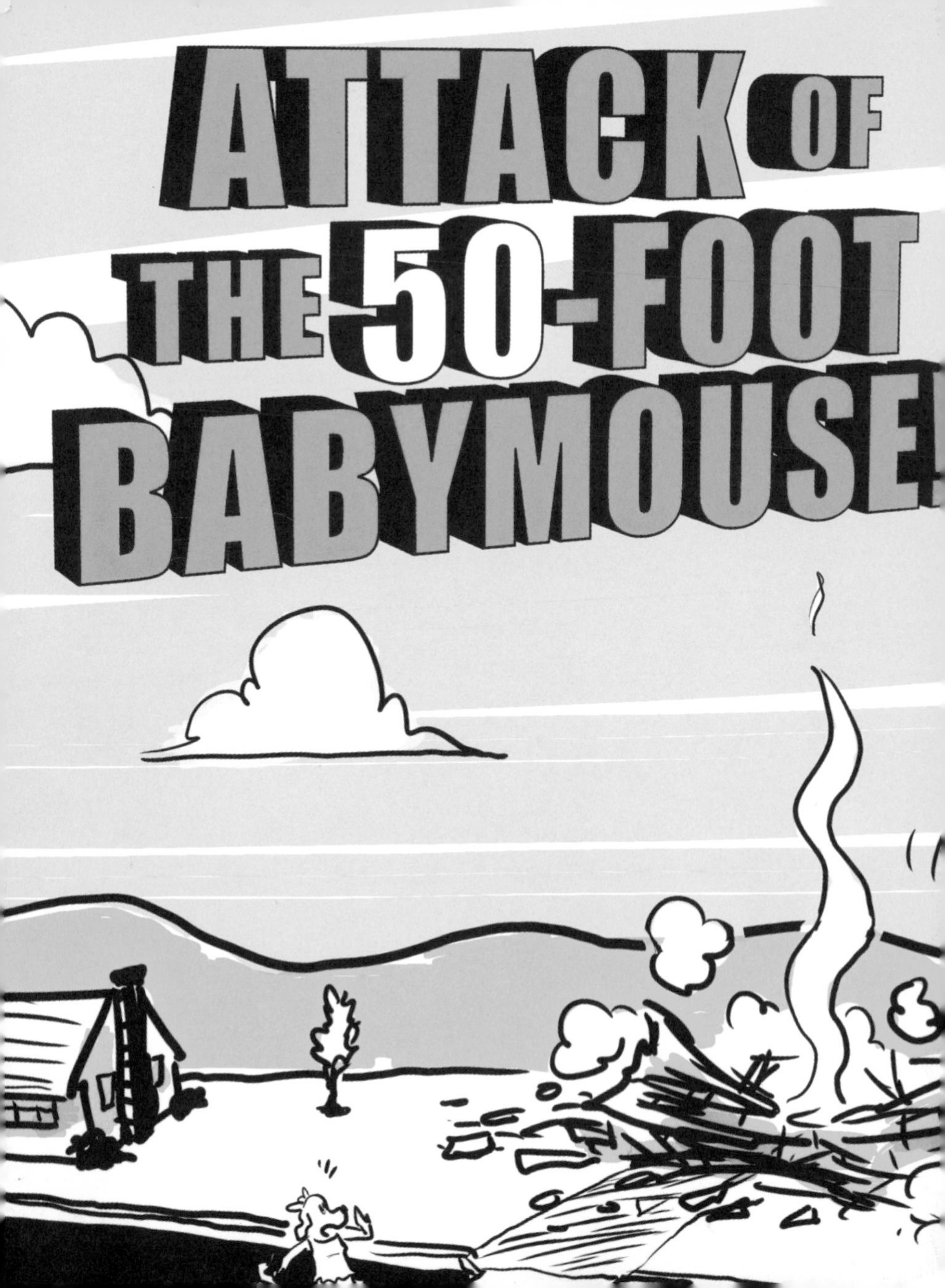
ATTACK OF THE 50-FOOT BABYMOUSE!

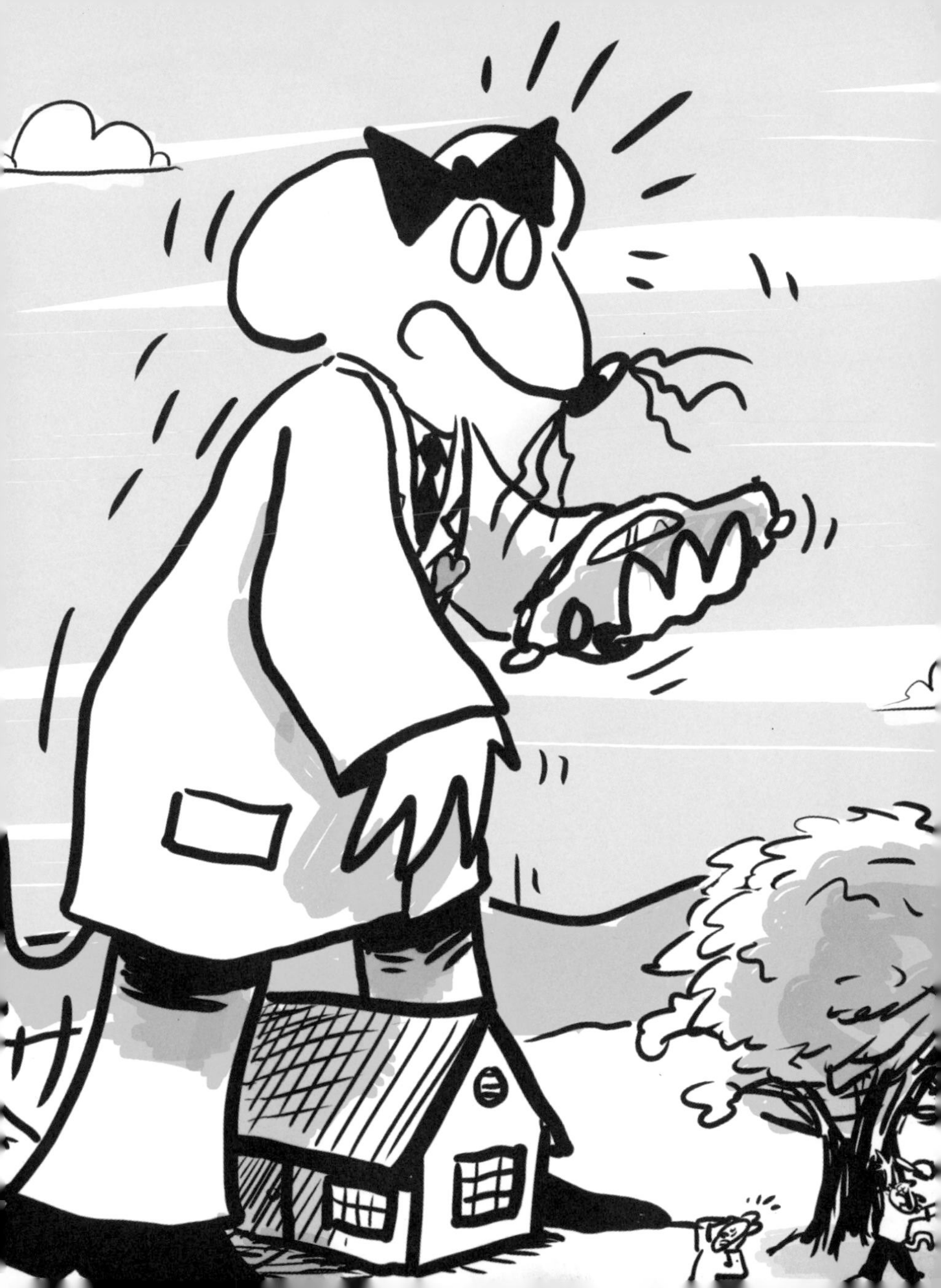

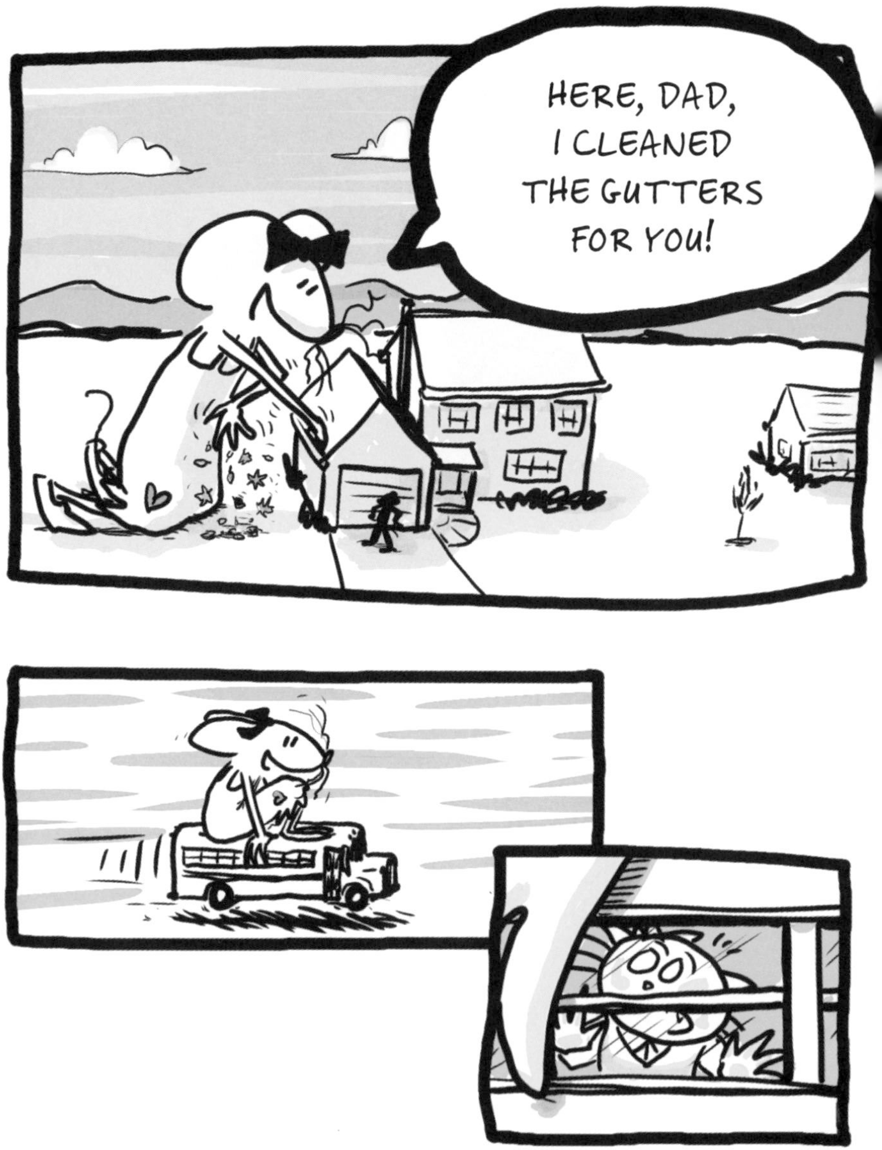
HERE, DAD, I CLEANED THE GUTTERS FOR YOU!

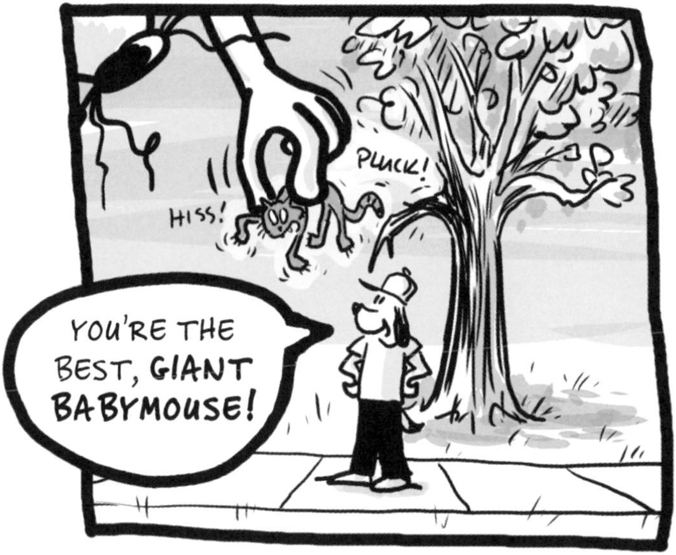
PLUCK!
HISS!
YOU'RE THE BEST, GIANT BABYMOUSE!

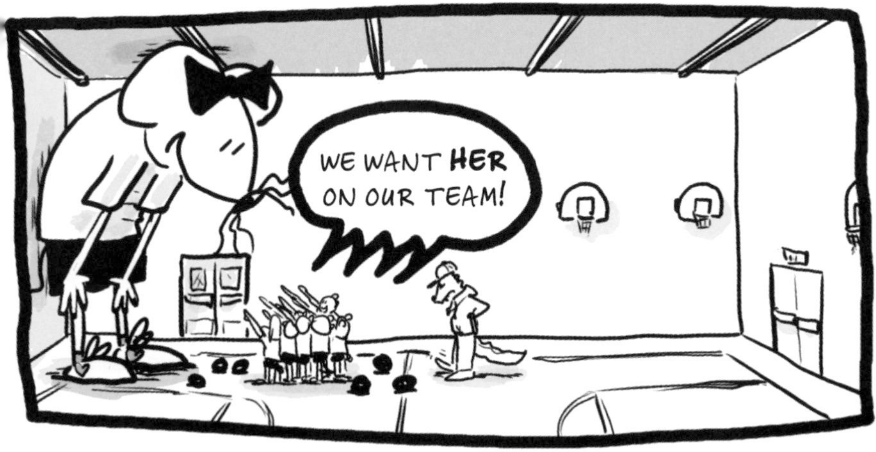
WE WANT HER ON OUR TEAM!

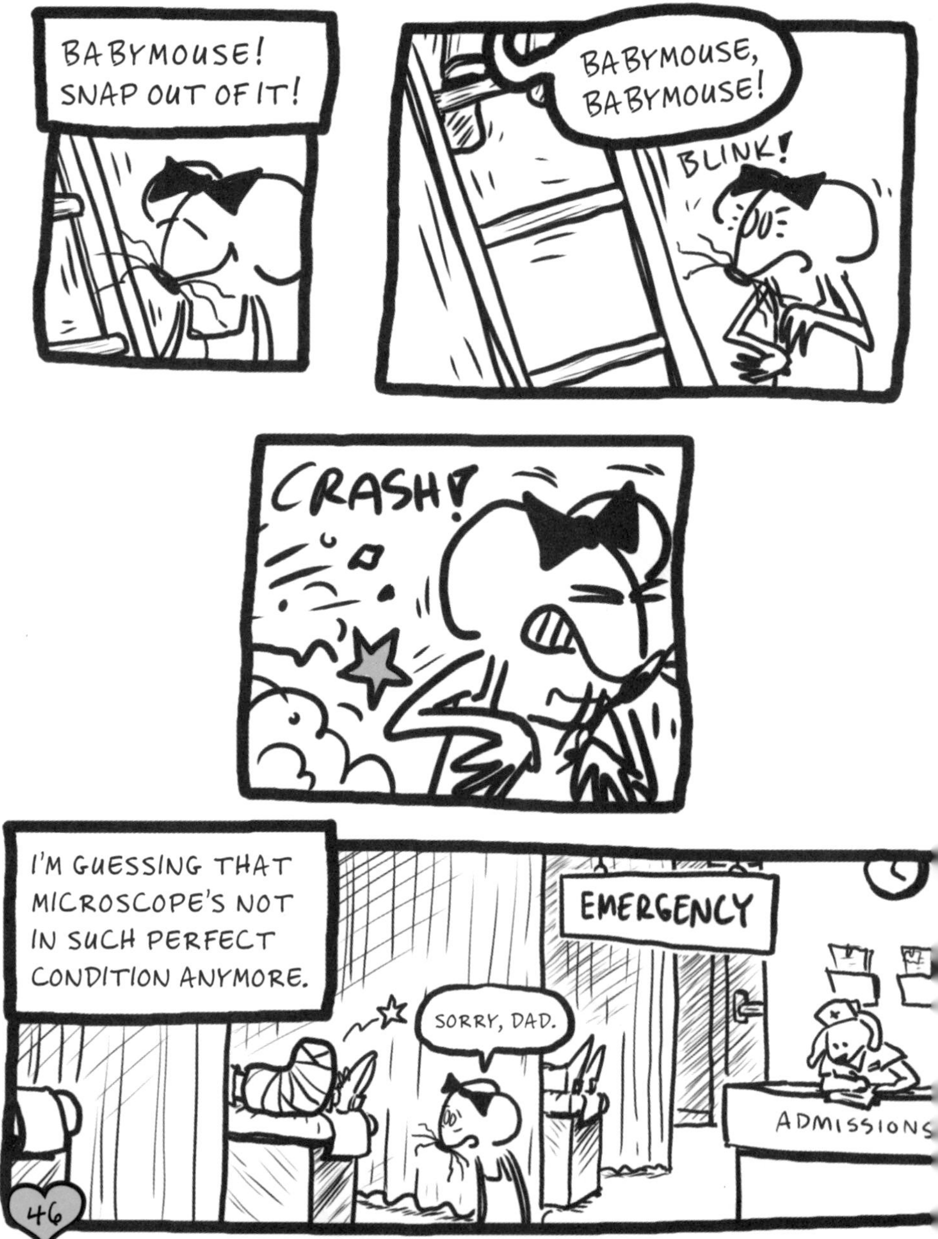
BABYMOUSE! SNAP OUT OF IT!
BABYMOUSE, BABYMOUSE!
BLINK!
CRASH!
I'M GUESSING THAT MICROSCOPE'S NOT IN SUCH PERFECT CONDITION ANYMORE.
EMERGENCY
SORRY, DAD.
ADMISSIONS

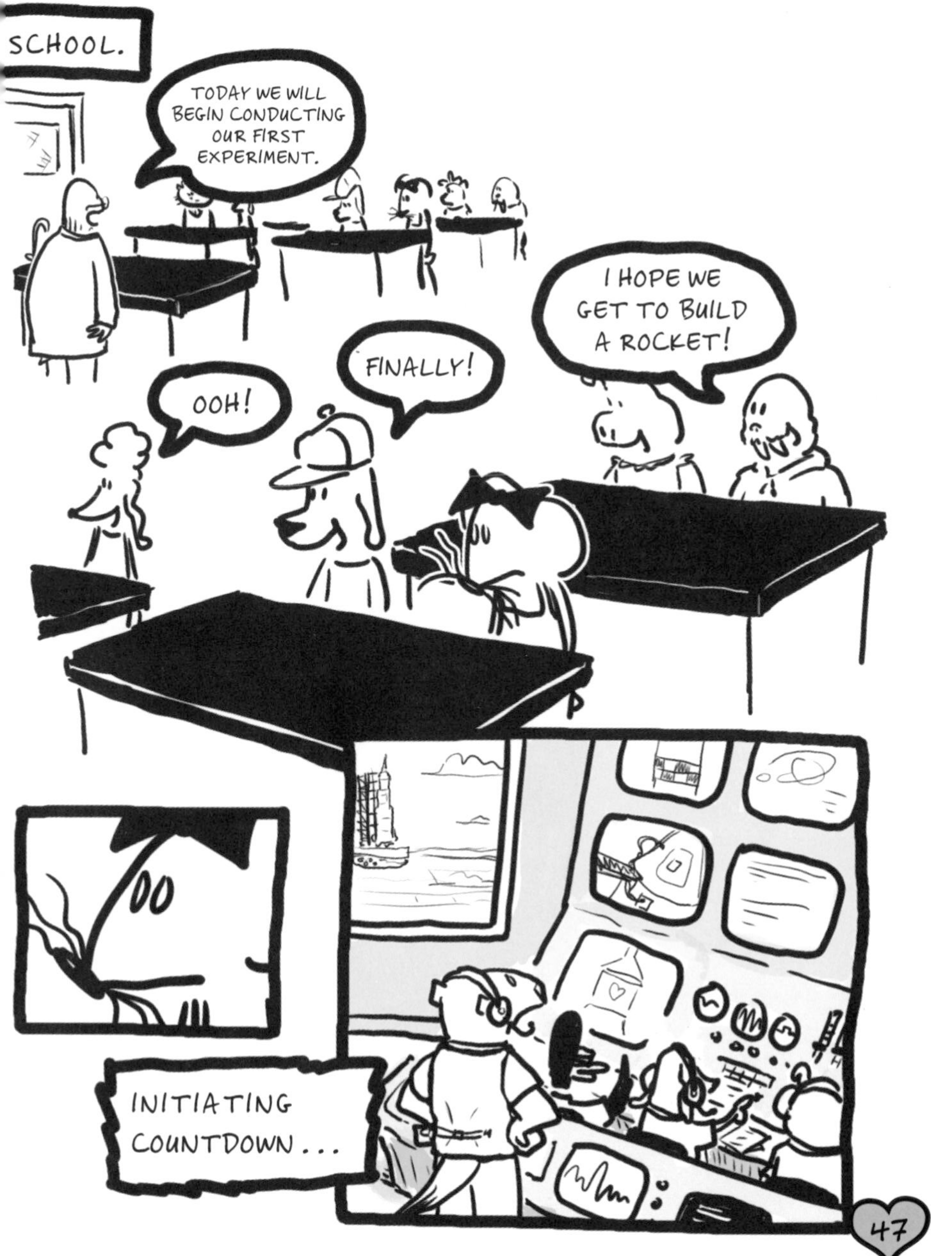
SCHOOL.
TODAY WE WILL BEGIN CONDUCTING OUR FIRST EXPERIMENT.
OOH!
FINALLY!
I HOPE WE GET TO BUILD A ROCKET!
INITIATING COUNTDOWN . . .

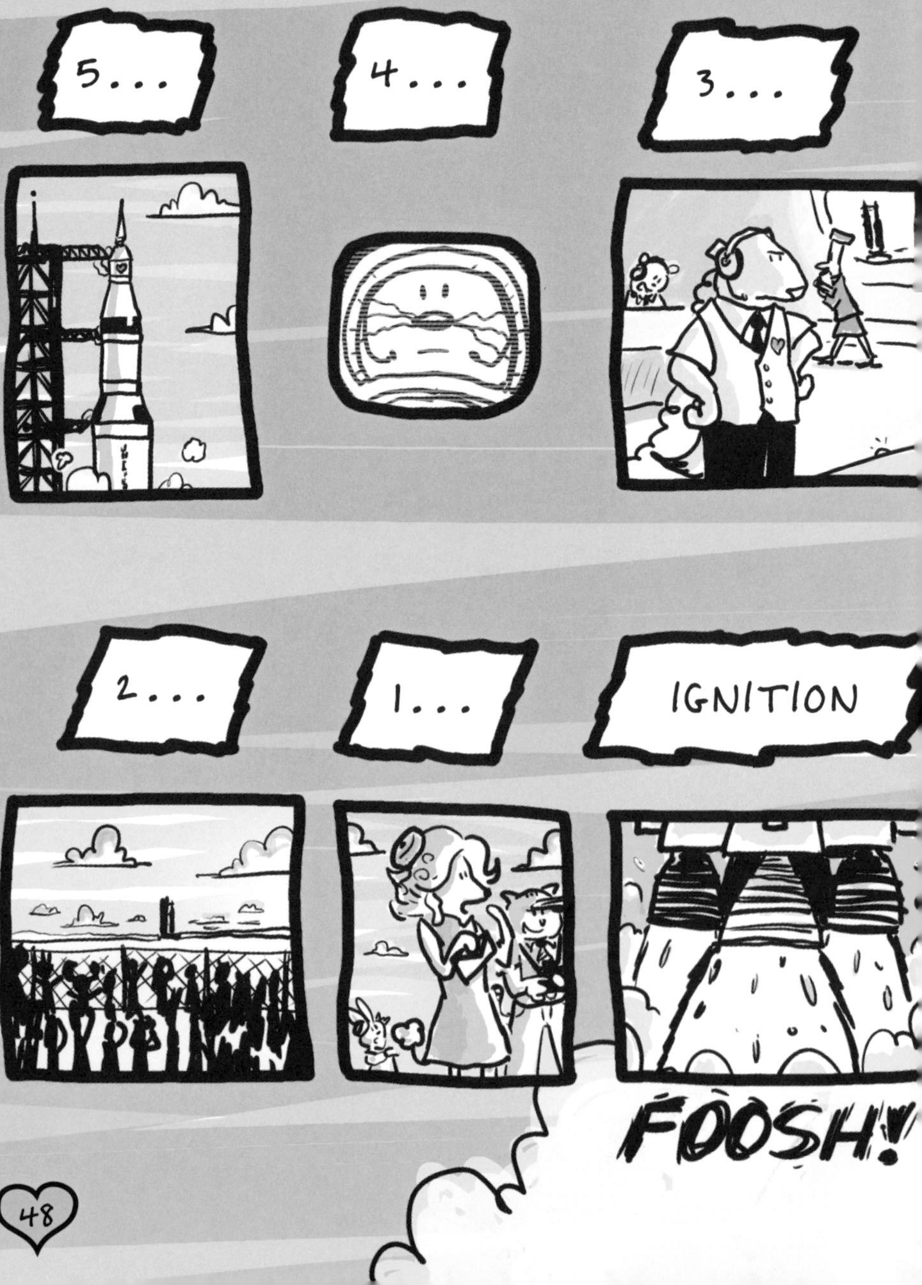
5...
4...
3...
2...
1...
IGNITION
FOOSH!

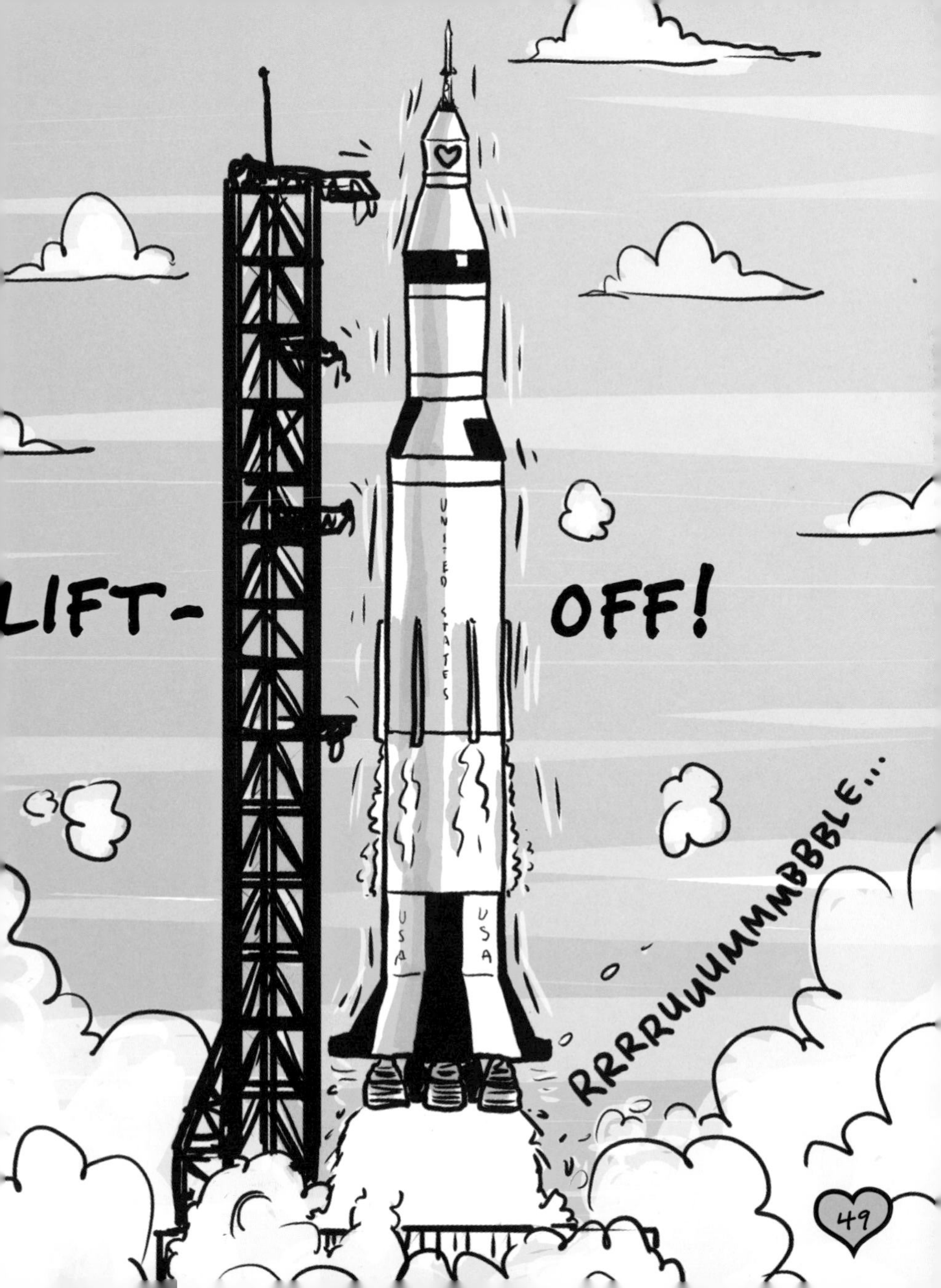
LIFT-
OFF!
UNITED STATES
USA
USA
RRRRUUUUMMMBBBLE...

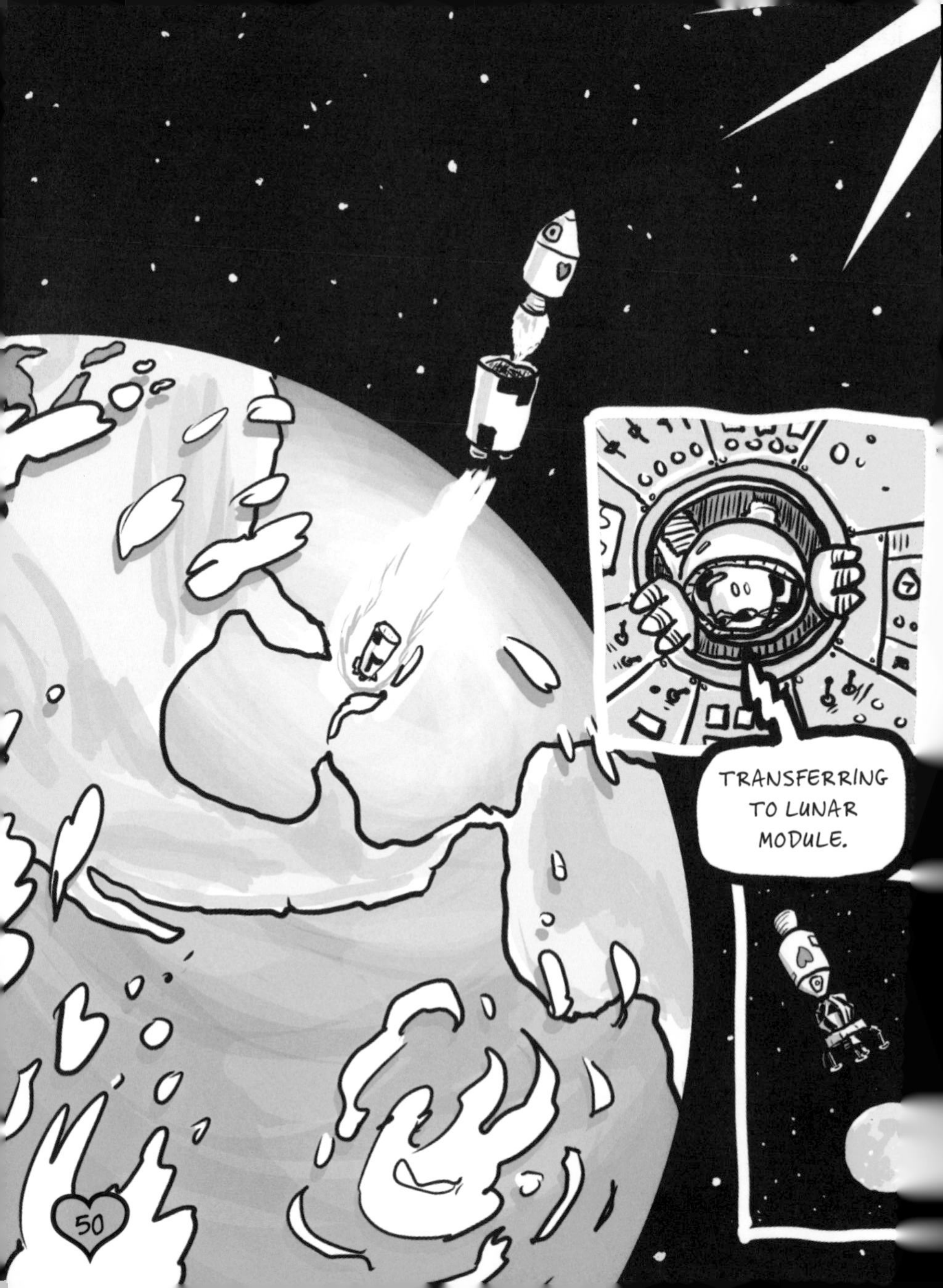
TRANSFERRING TO LUNAR MODULE.
50

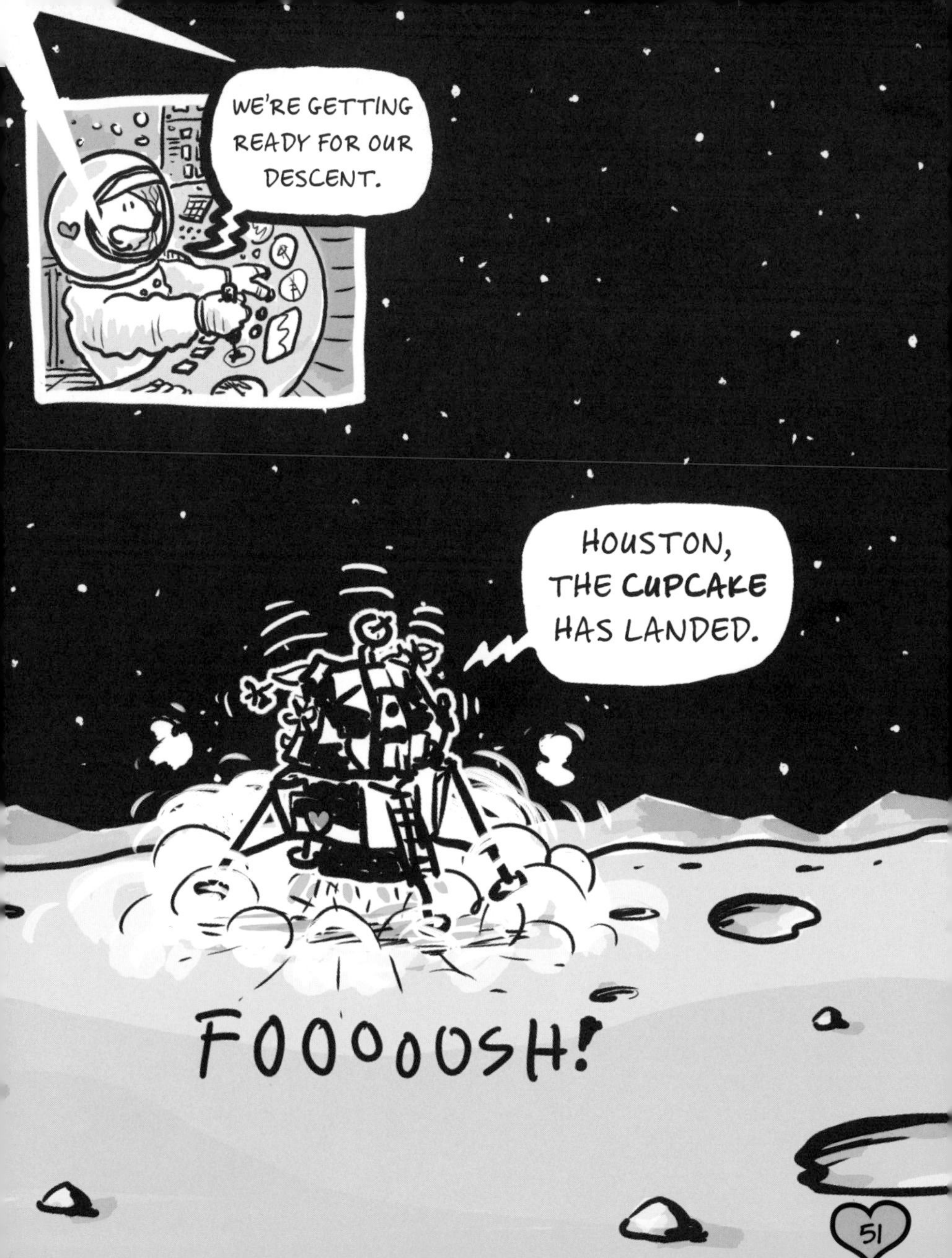
WE'RE GETTING READY FOR OUR DESCENT.
HOUSTON, THE **CUPCAKE** HAS LANDED.
FOOOOOSH!

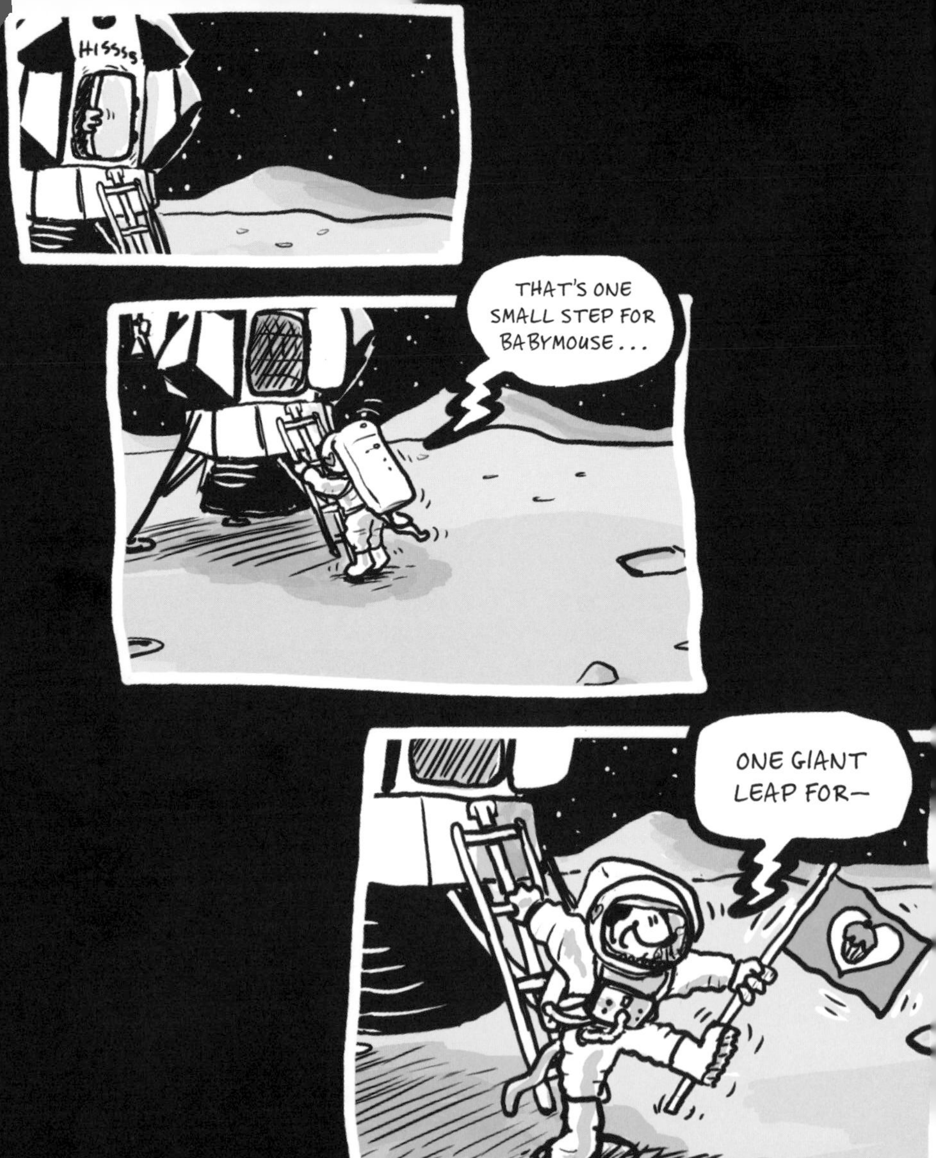
HISSSS
THAT'S ONE SMALL STEP FOR BABYMOUSE...
ONE GIANT LEAP FOR—

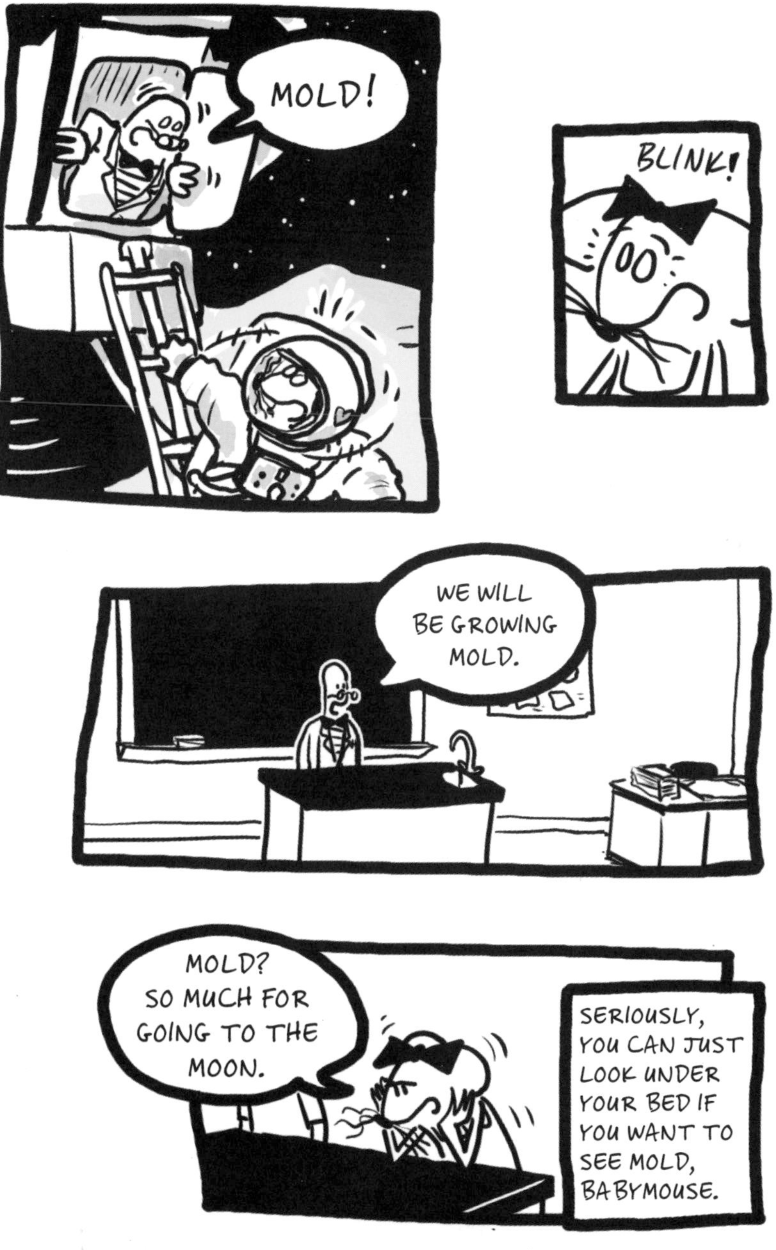
MOLD!
BLINK!
WE WILL BE GROWING MOLD.
MOLD? SO MUCH FOR GOING TO THE MOON.
SERIOUSLY, YOU CAN JUST LOOK UNDER YOUR BED IF YOU WANT TO SEE MOLD, BABYMOUSE.

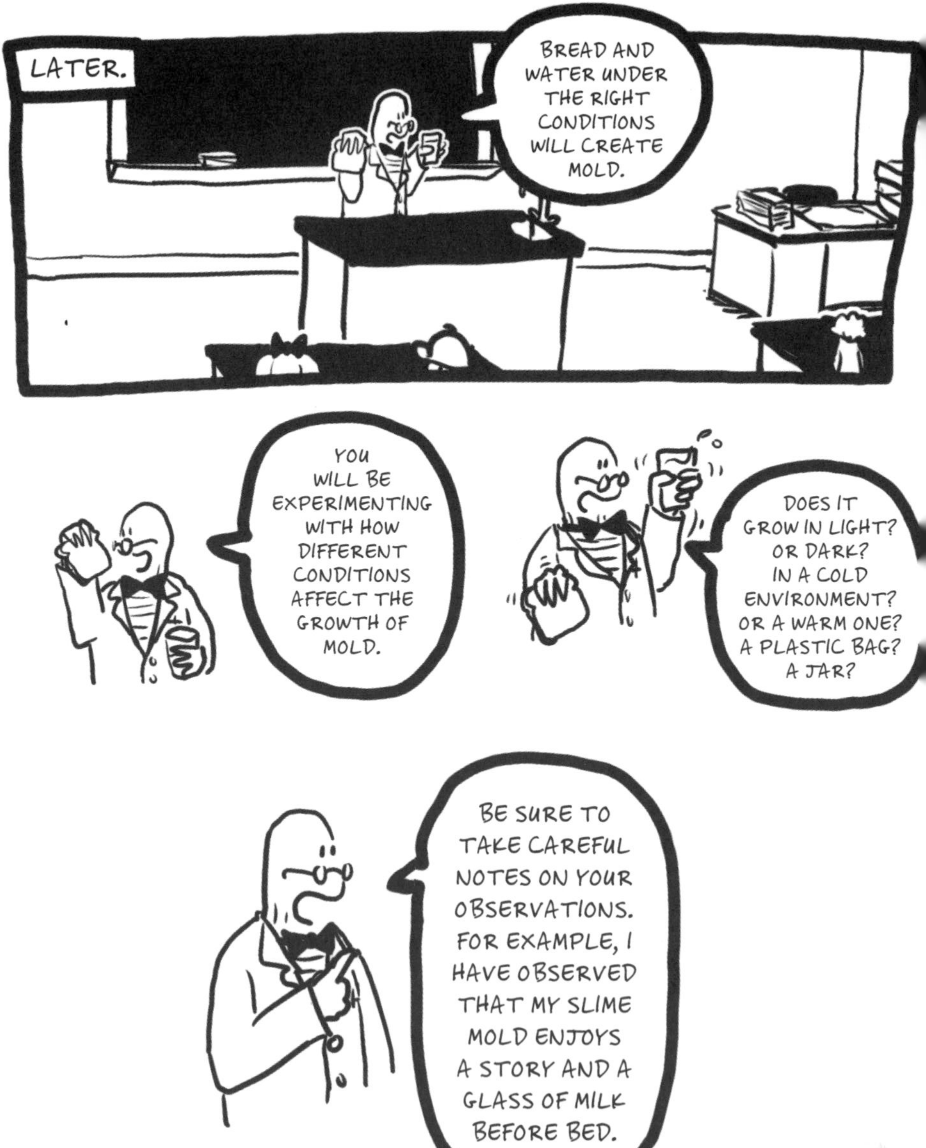

LATER.
BREAD AND WATER UNDER THE RIGHT CONDITIONS WILL CREATE MOLD.
YOU WILL BE EXPERIMENTING WITH HOW DIFFERENT CONDITIONS AFFECT THE GROWTH OF MOLD.
DOES IT GROW IN LIGHT? OR DARK? IN A COLD ENVIRONMENT? OR A WARM ONE? A PLASTIC BAG? A JAR?
BE SURE TO TAKE CAREFUL NOTES ON YOUR OBSERVATIONS. FOR EXAMPLE, I HAVE OBSERVED THAT MY SLIME MOLD ENJOYS A STORY AND A GLASS OF MILK BEFORE BED.

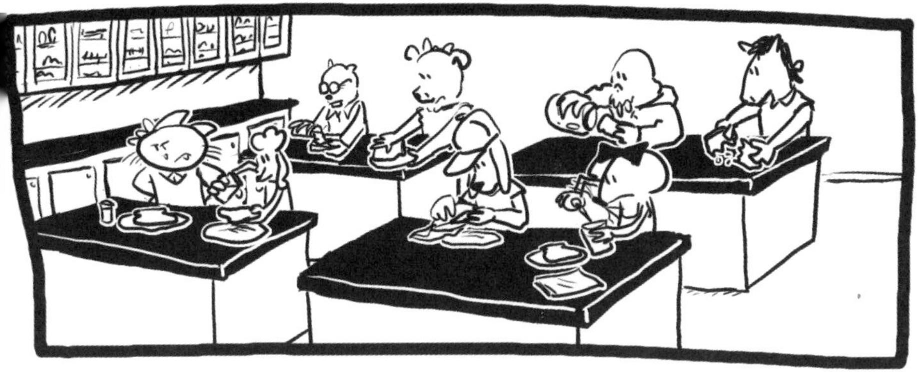

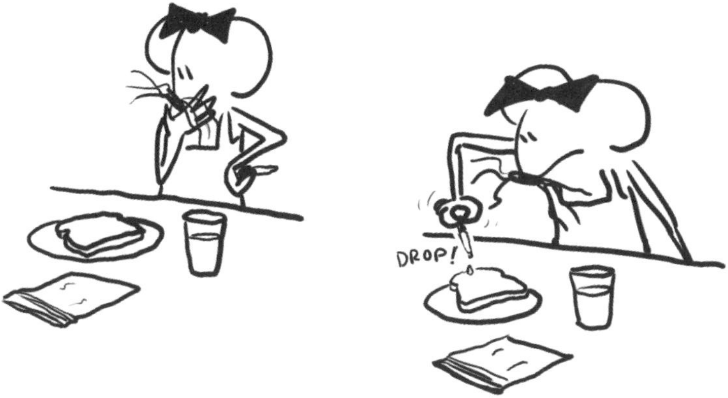
DROP!

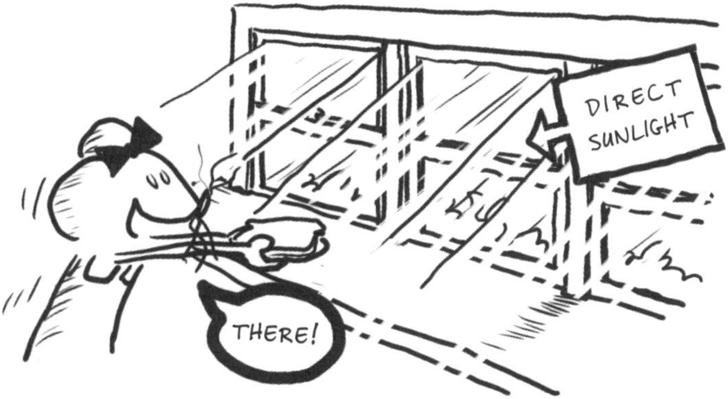
DIRECT SUNLIGHT
THERE!

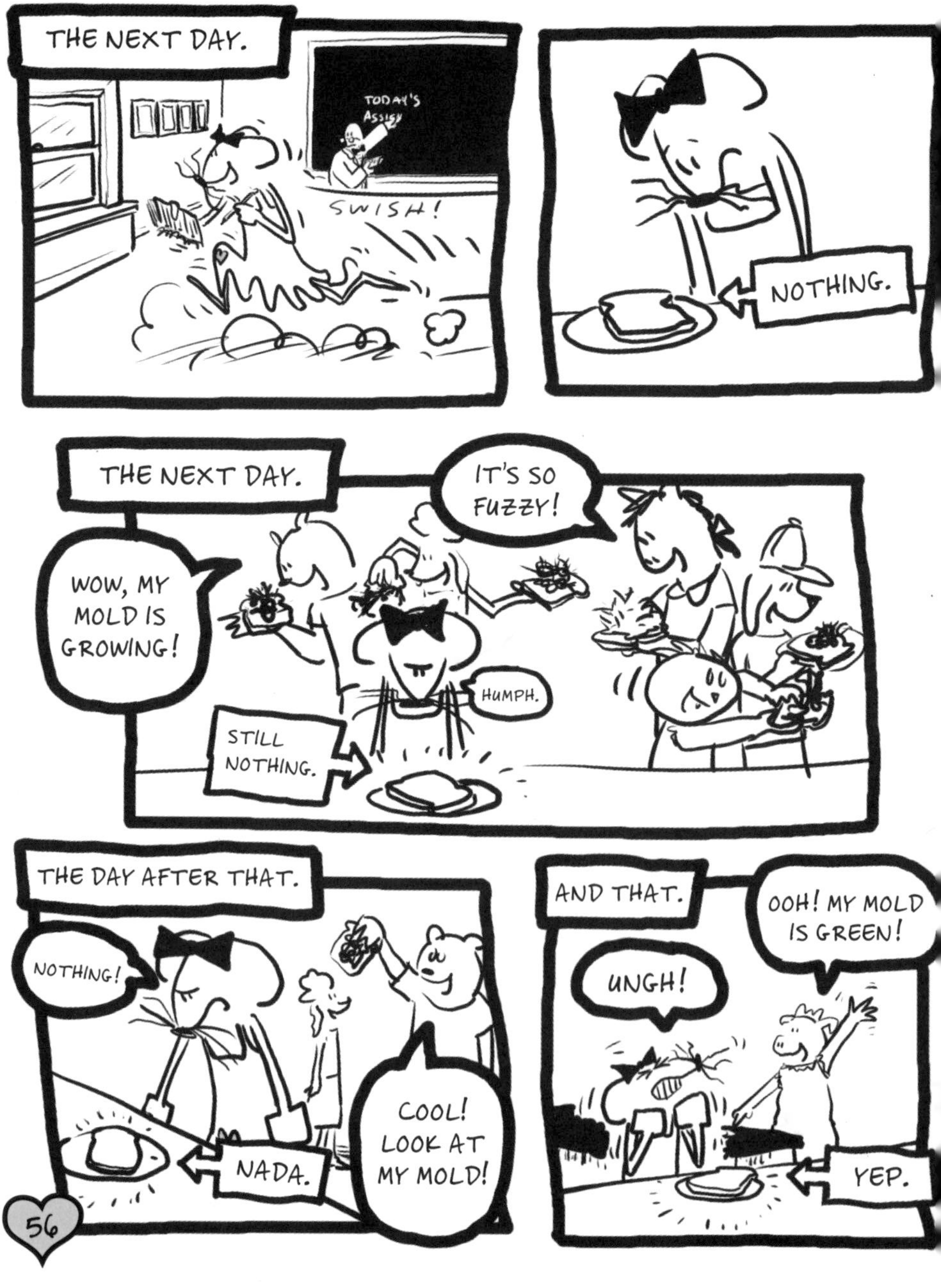
THE NEXT DAY.
TODAY'S ASSIGN
SWISH!
NOTHING.
THE NEXT DAY.
WOW, MY MOLD IS GROWING!
IT'S SO FUZZY!
HUMPH.
STILL NOTHING.
THE DAY AFTER THAT.
NOTHING!
NADA.
COOL! LOOK AT MY MOLD!
AND THAT.
OOH! MY MOLD IS GREEN!
UNGH!
YEP.

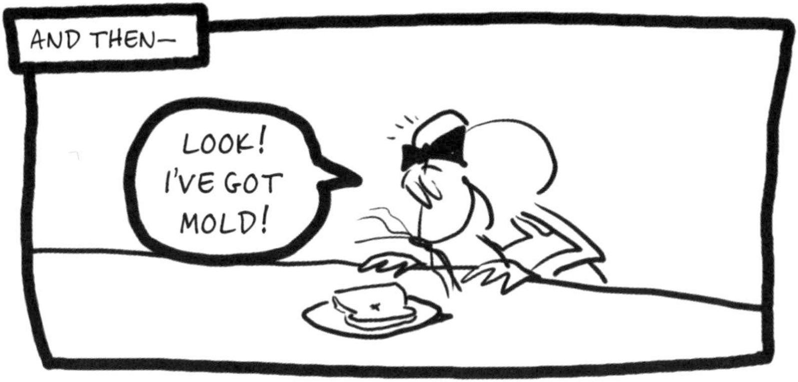
AND THEN—
LOOK! I'VE GOT MOLD!

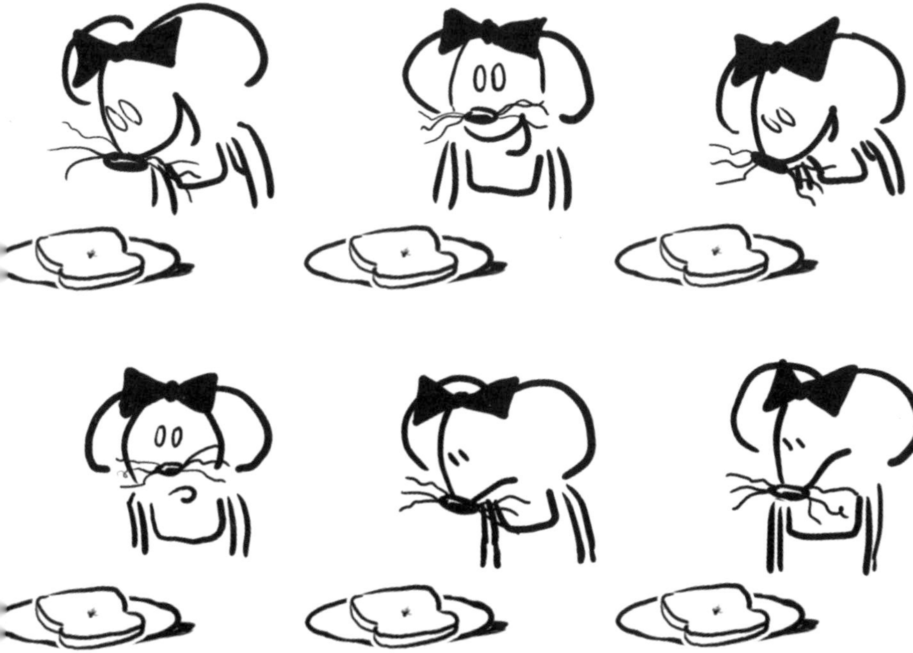

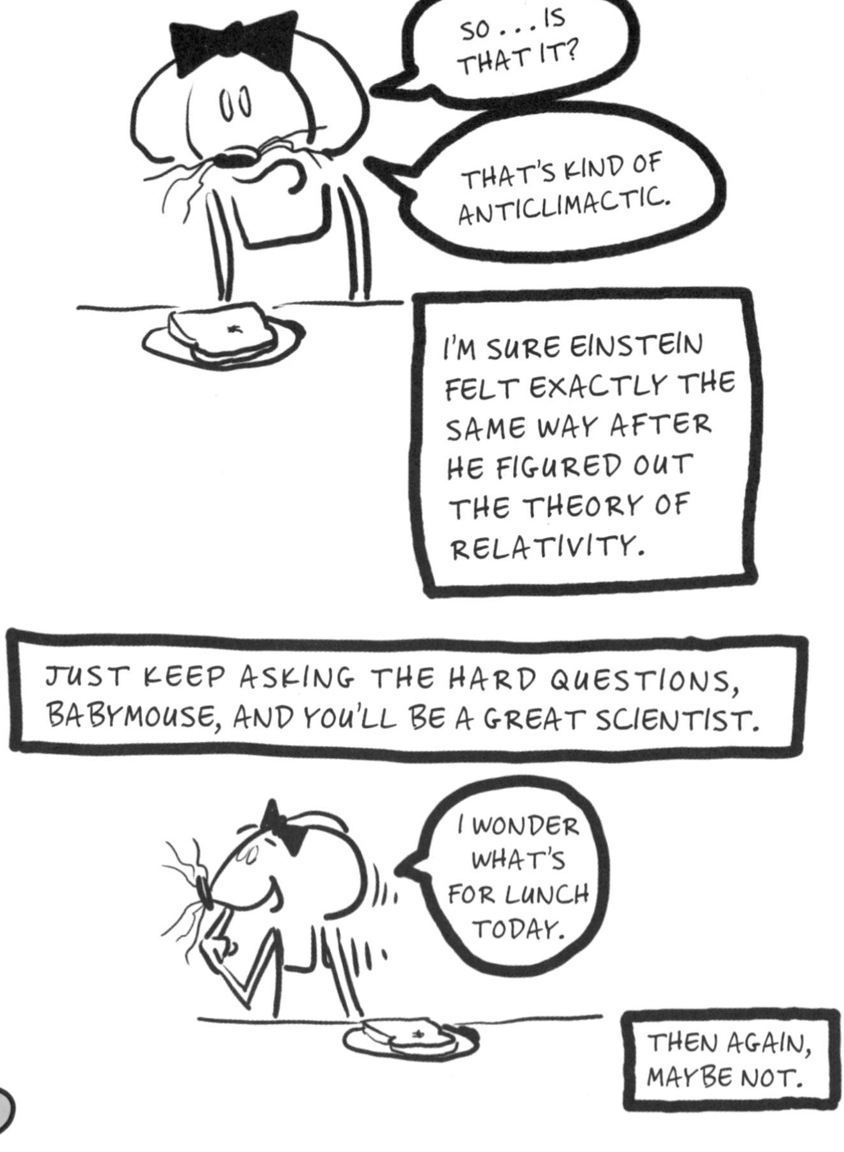

SO . . . IS THAT IT?
THAT'S KIND OF ANTICLIMACTIC.
I'M SURE EINSTEIN FELT EXACTLY THE SAME WAY AFTER HE FIGURED OUT THE THEORY OF RELATIVITY.
JUST KEEP ASKING THE HARD QUESTIONS, BABYMOUSE, AND YOU'LL BE A GREAT SCIENTIST.
I WONDER WHAT'S FOR LUNCH TODAY.
THEN AGAIN, MAYBE NOT.

SATURDAY.

I LOVE WEEKENDS!

SPROING!

ANY BIG PLANS TODAY, BABYMOUSE?

MORNING, BABYMOUSE! I GOT YOU A PRESENT!

IS IT ANOTHER BOOK?

NO, BABYMOUSE. IT'S EVEN BETTER THAN A BOOK.

A MICROSCOPE!

JUNIOR MICROSCOPE JUNIOR MICROSCOPE

IT'S JUST LIKE THE ONE I HAD WHEN I WAS A KID.

WOW! IT'S EVEN NICER THAN THE ONE THAT BROKE WHEN YOUR DAD FELL OFF THE LADDER, BABYMOUSE.

JUNIOR MICROSCOPE JUNIOR MICROSCOPE

RUB IT IN, WHY DON'TCHA?

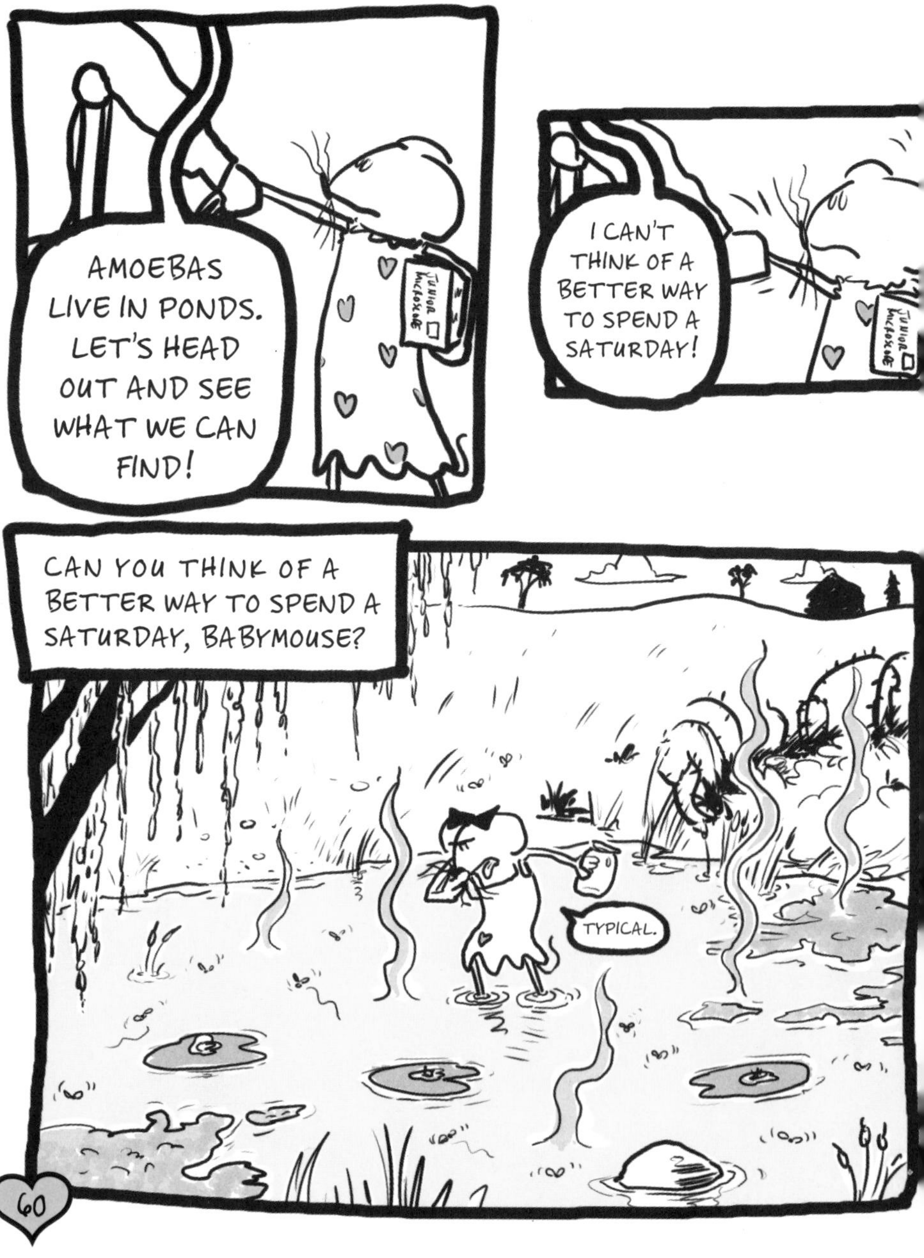
AMOEBAS LIVE IN PONDS. LET'S HEAD OUT AND SEE WHAT WE CAN FIND!
I CAN'T THINK OF A BETTER WAY TO SPEND A SATURDAY!
CAN YOU THINK OF A BETTER WAY TO SPEND A SATURDAY, BABYMOUSE?
TYPICAL.

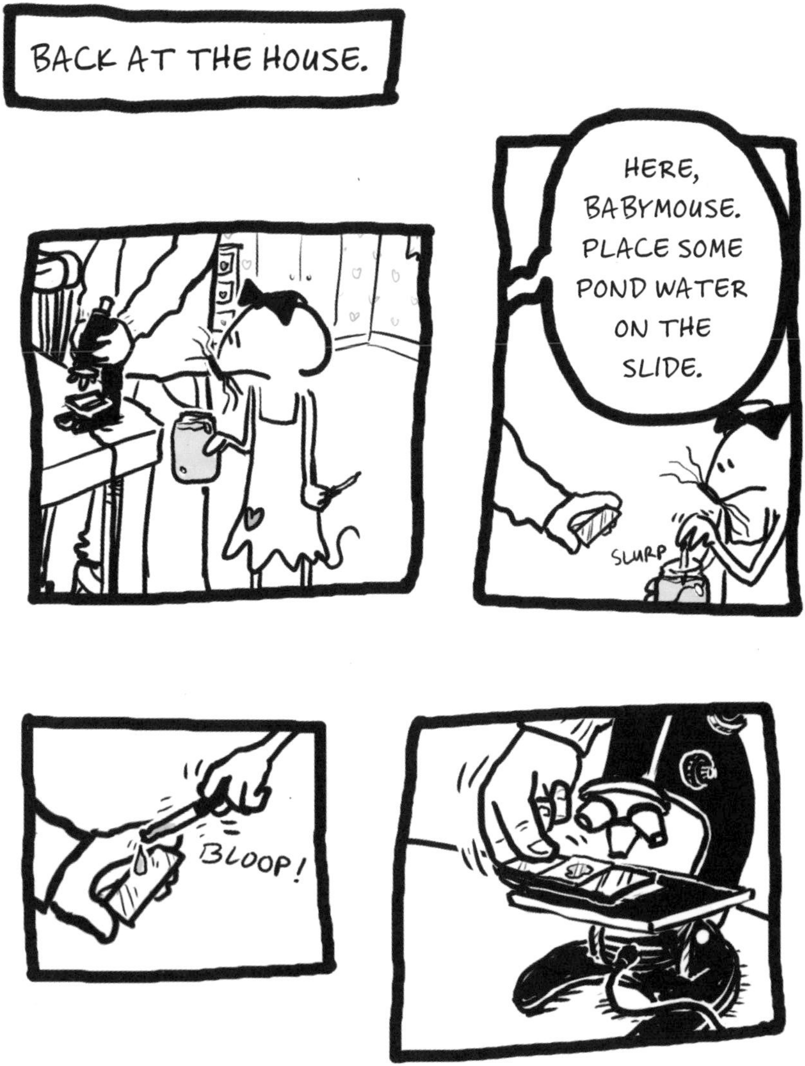
BACK AT THE HOUSE.
HERE, BABYMOUSE. PLACE SOME POND WATER ON THE SLIDE.
SLURP
BLOOP!

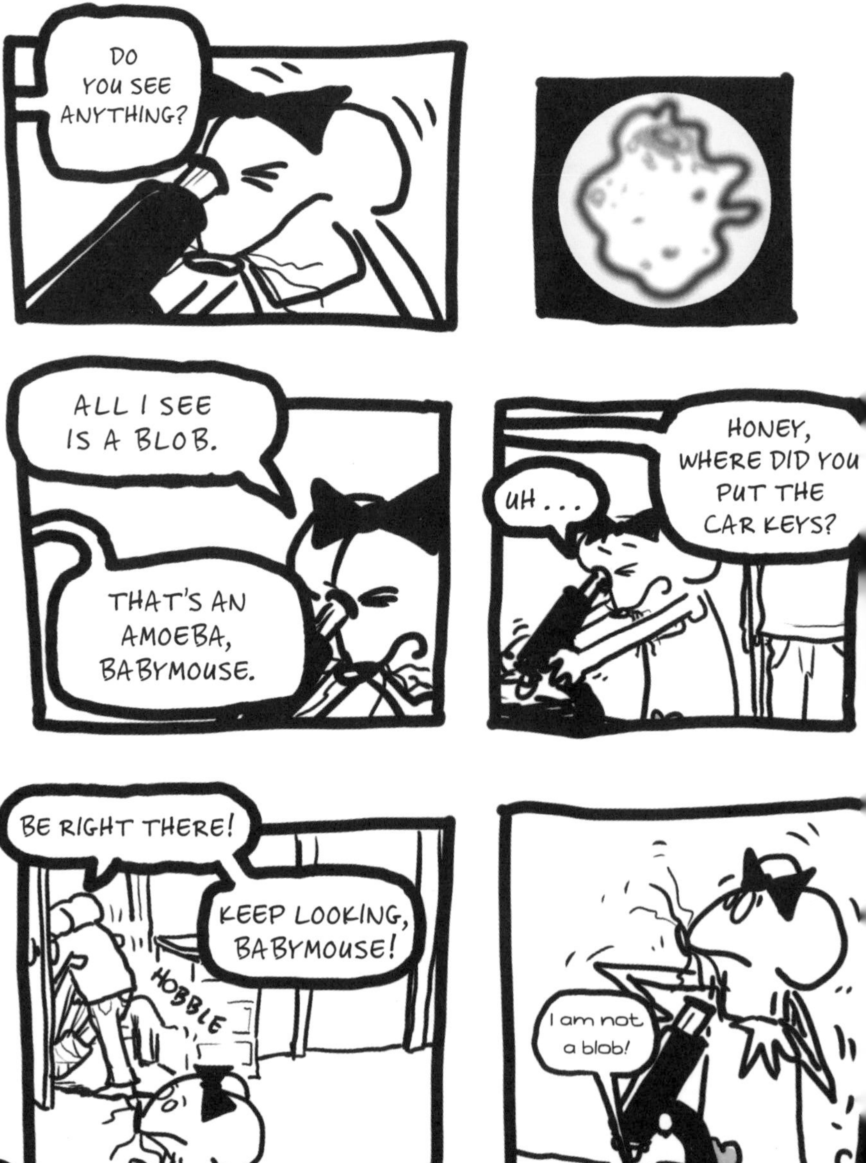
DO YOU SEE ANYTHING?
ALL I SEE IS A BLOB.
THAT'S AN AMOEBA, BABYMOUSE.
HONEY, WHERE DID YOU PUT THE CAR KEYS?
UH . . .
BE RIGHT THERE!
KEEP LOOKING, BABYMOUSE!
HOBBLE
I am not a blob!

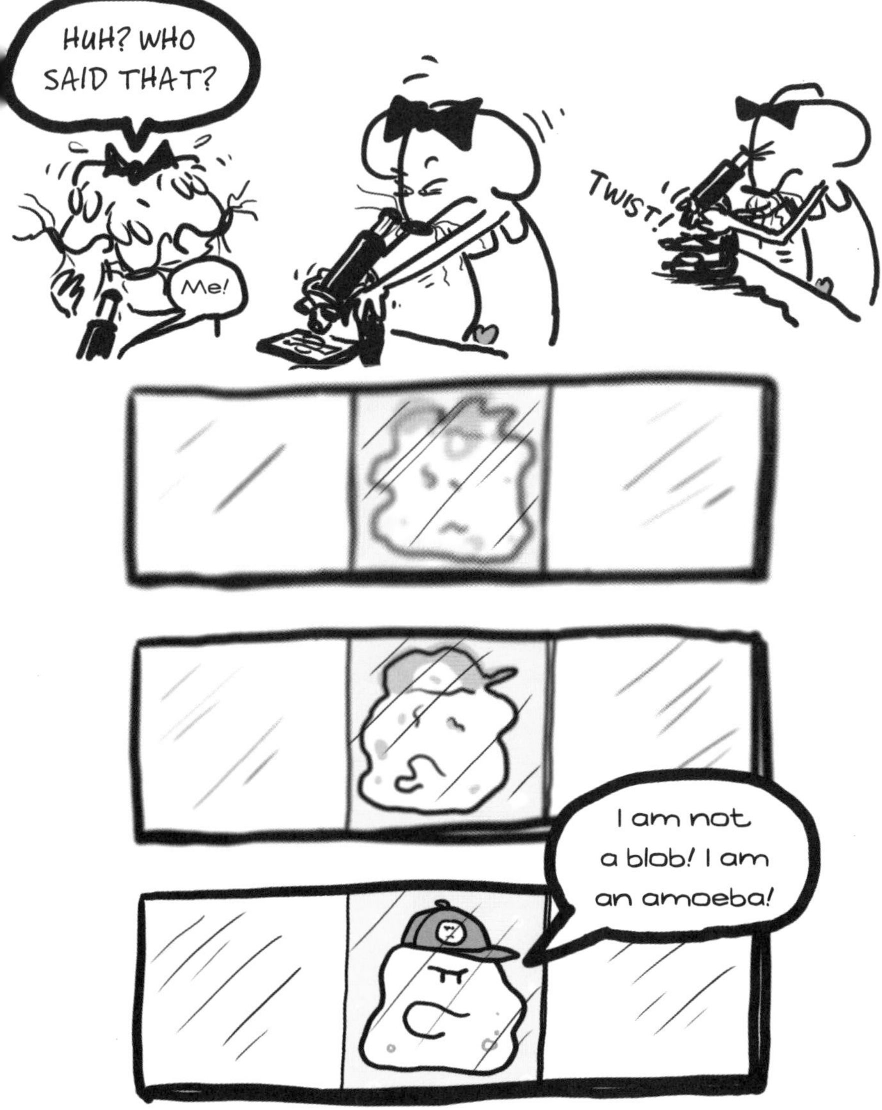
HUH? WHO SAID THAT?
Me!
TWIST!
I am not a blob! I am an amoeba!

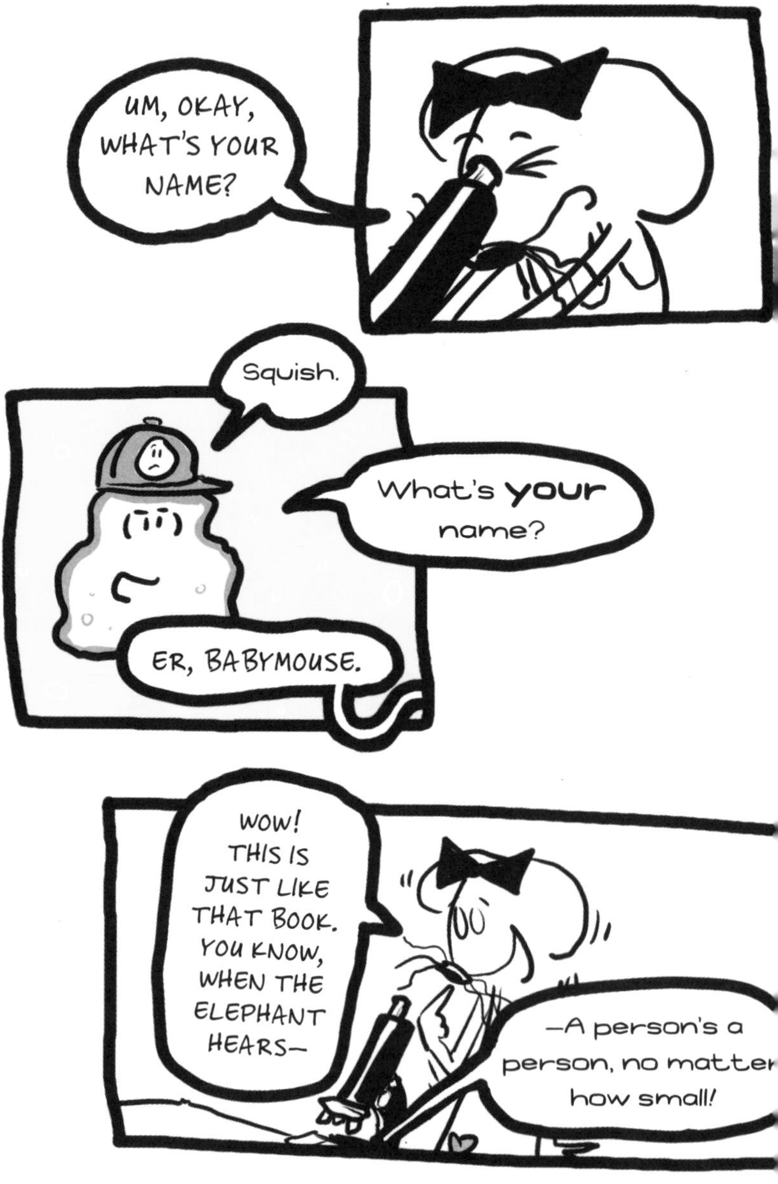
UM, OKAY, WHAT'S YOUR NAME?
Squish.
What's **your** name?
ER, BABYMOUSE.
WOW! THIS IS JUST LIKE THAT BOOK. YOU KNOW, WHEN THE ELEPHANT HEARS—
—A person's a person, no matter how small!

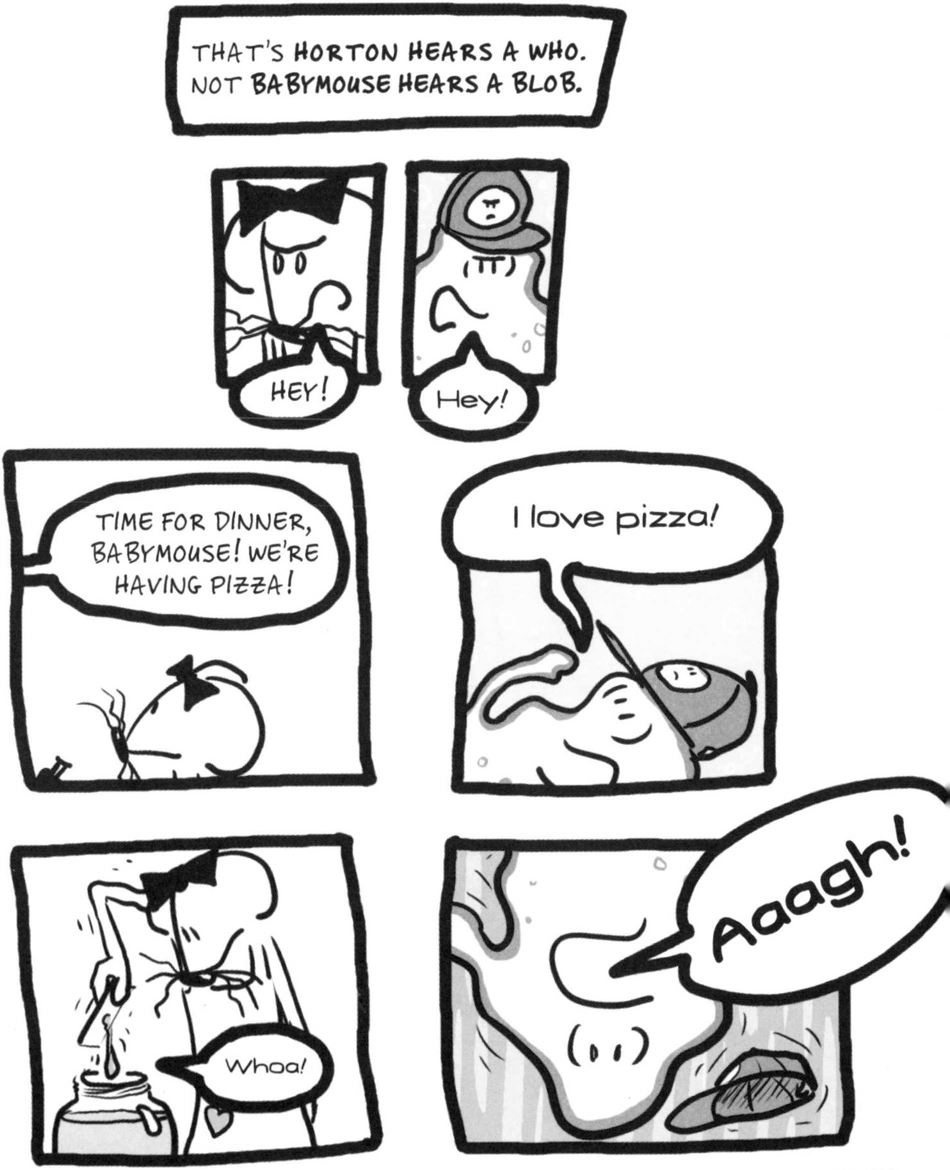
THAT'S HORTON HEARS A WHO.
NOT BABYMOUSE HEARS A BLOB.
HEY!
Hey!
TIME FOR DINNER, BABYMOUSE! WE'RE HAVING PIZZA!
I love pizza!
Whoa!
Aaagh!

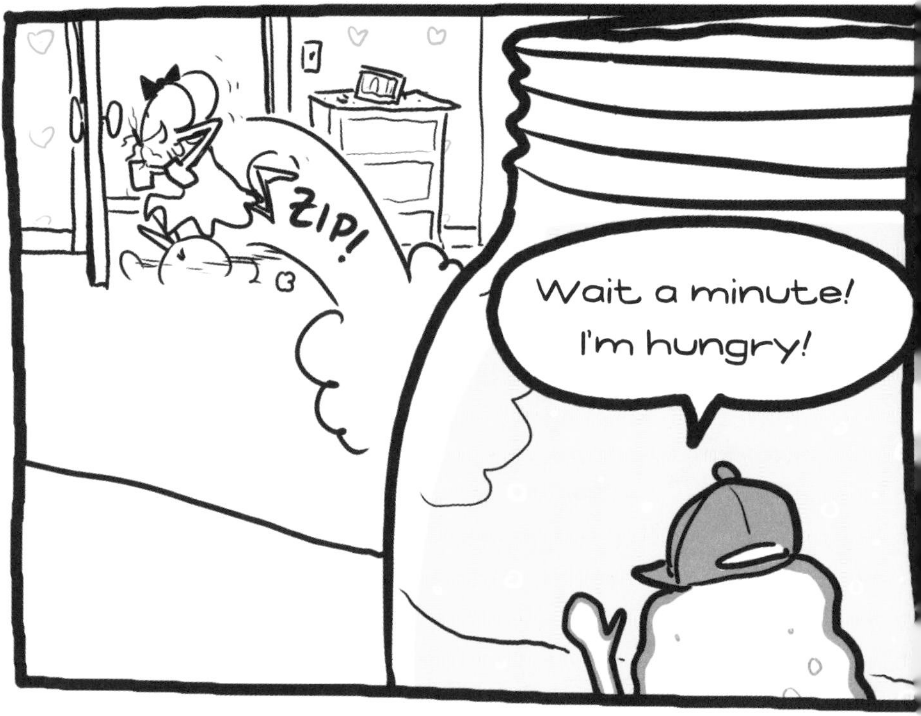
ZIP!
Wait a minute! I'm hungry!

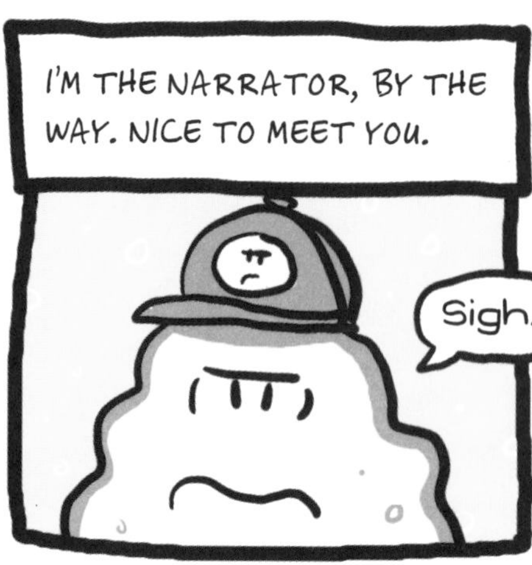
I'M THE NARRATOR, BY THE WAY. NICE TO MEET YOU.
Sigh.

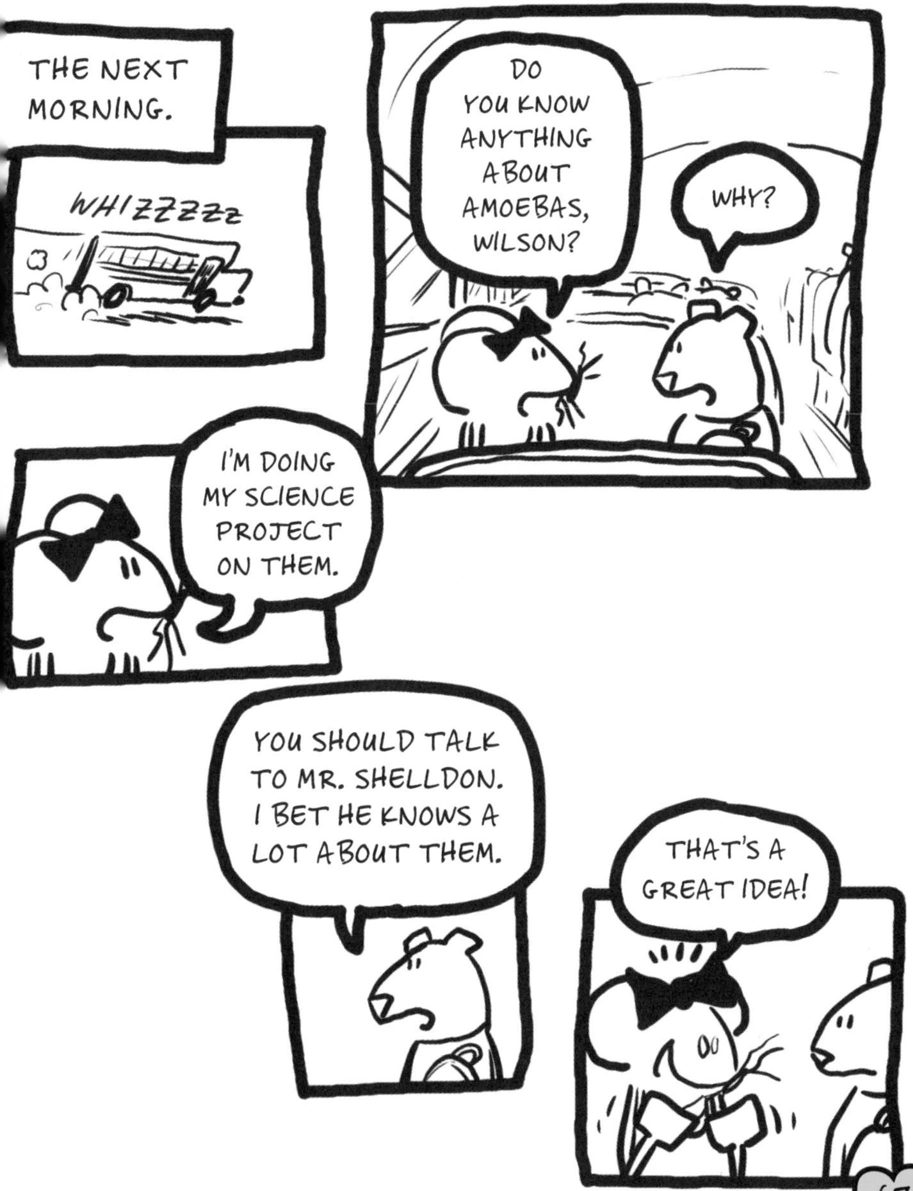
THE NEXT MORNING.
WHIZZZZZ
DO YOU KNOW ANYTHING ABOUT AMOEBAS, WILSON?
WHY?
I'M DOING MY SCIENCE PROJECT ON THEM.
YOU SHOULD TALK TO MR. SHELLDON. I BET HE KNOWS A LOT ABOUT THEM.
THAT'S A GREAT IDEA!

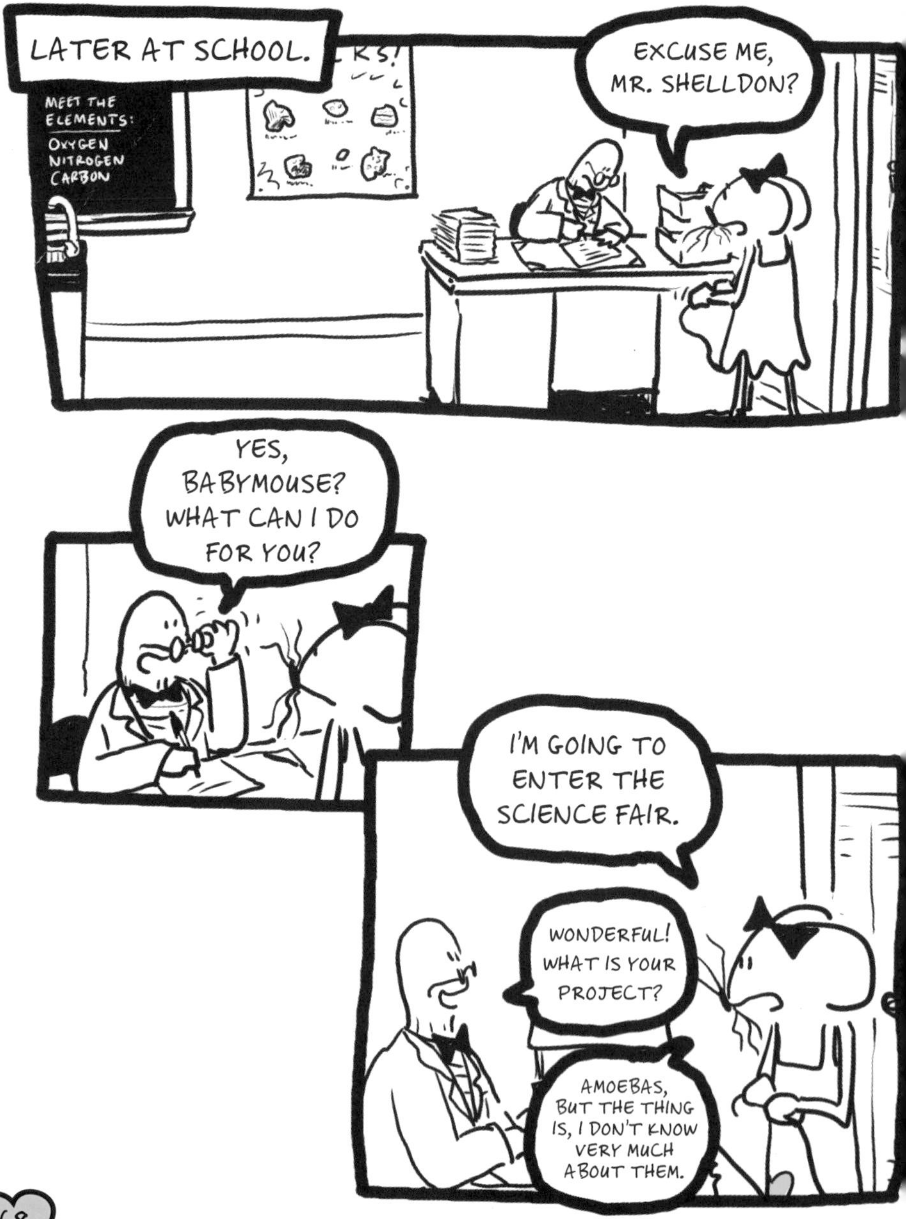
LATER AT SCHOOL.
MEET THE ELEMENTS:
OXYGEN
NITROGEN
CARBON
EXCUSE ME, MR. SHELLDON?
YES, BABYMOUSE? WHAT CAN I DO FOR YOU?
I'M GOING TO ENTER THE SCIENCE FAIR.
WONDERFUL! WHAT IS YOUR PROJECT?
AMOEBAS, BUT THE THING IS, I DON'T KNOW VERY MUCH ABOUT THEM.

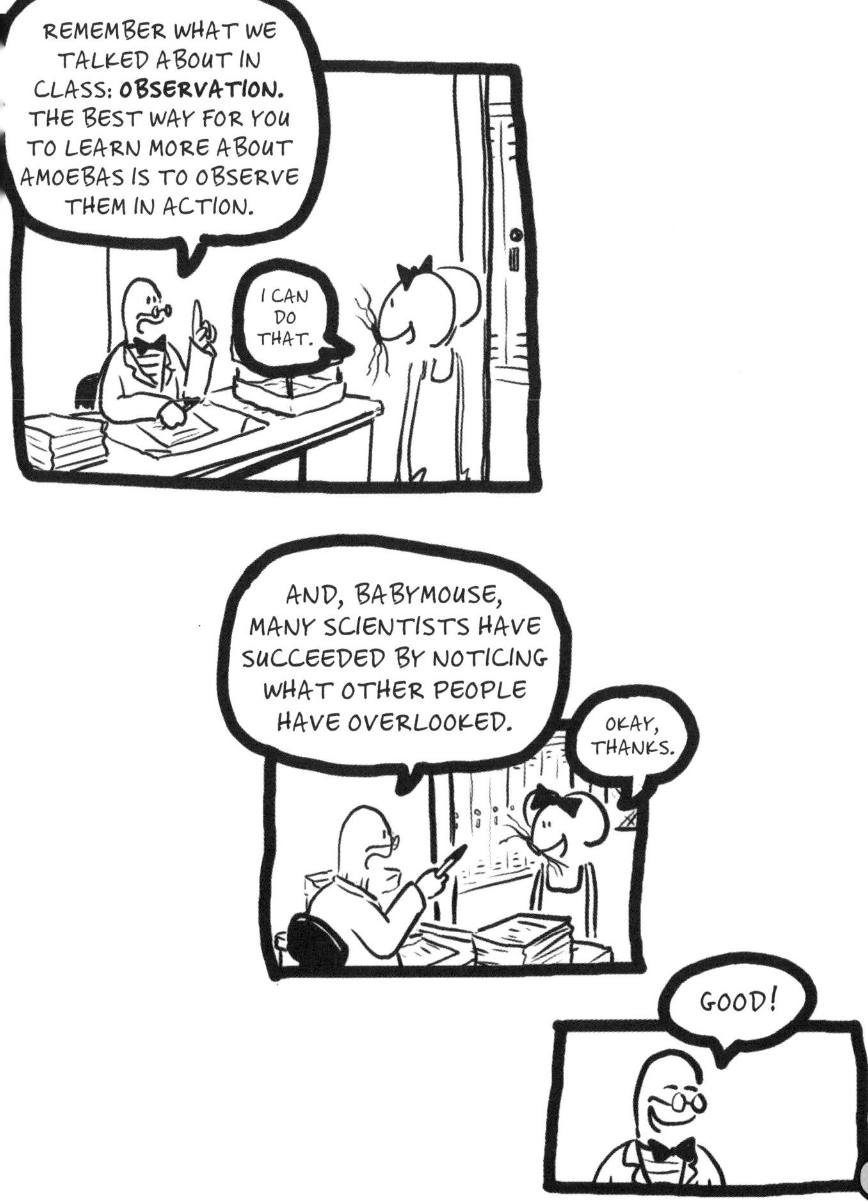
REMEMBER WHAT WE TALKED ABOUT IN CLASS: **OBSERVATION.** THE BEST WAY FOR YOU TO LEARN MORE ABOUT AMOEBAS IS TO OBSERVE THEM IN ACTION.
I CAN DO THAT.
AND, BABYMOUSE, MANY SCIENTISTS HAVE SUCCEEDED BY NOTICING WHAT OTHER PEOPLE HAVE OVERLOOKED.
OKAY, THANKS.
GOOD!

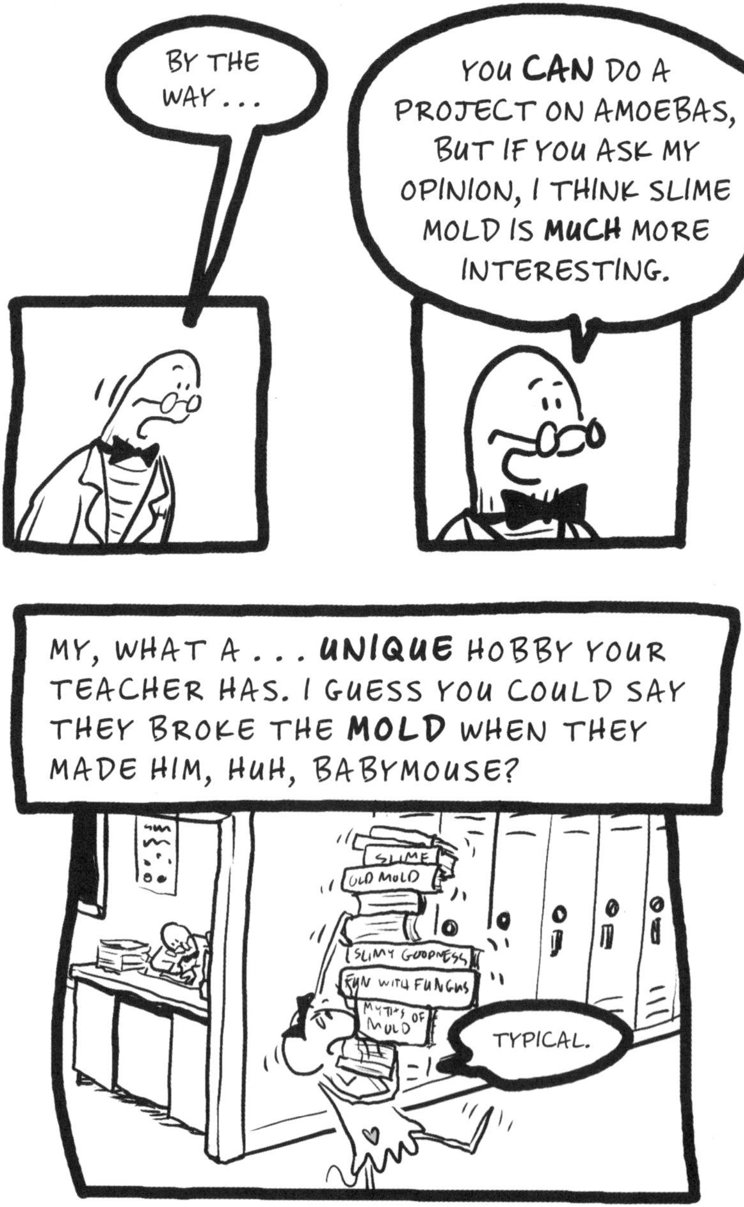
BY THE WAY . . .
YOU **CAN** DO A PROJECT ON AMOEBAS, BUT IF YOU ASK MY OPINION, I THINK SLIME MOLD IS **MUCH** MORE INTERESTING.
MY, WHAT A . . . **UNIQUE** HOBBY YOUR TEACHER HAS. I GUESS YOU COULD SAY THEY BROKE THE **MOLD** WHEN THEY MADE HIM, HUH, BABYMOUSE?
SLIME
OLD MOLD
SLIMY GOODNESS
FUN WITH FUNGUS
MYTHS OF MOLD
TYPICAL.

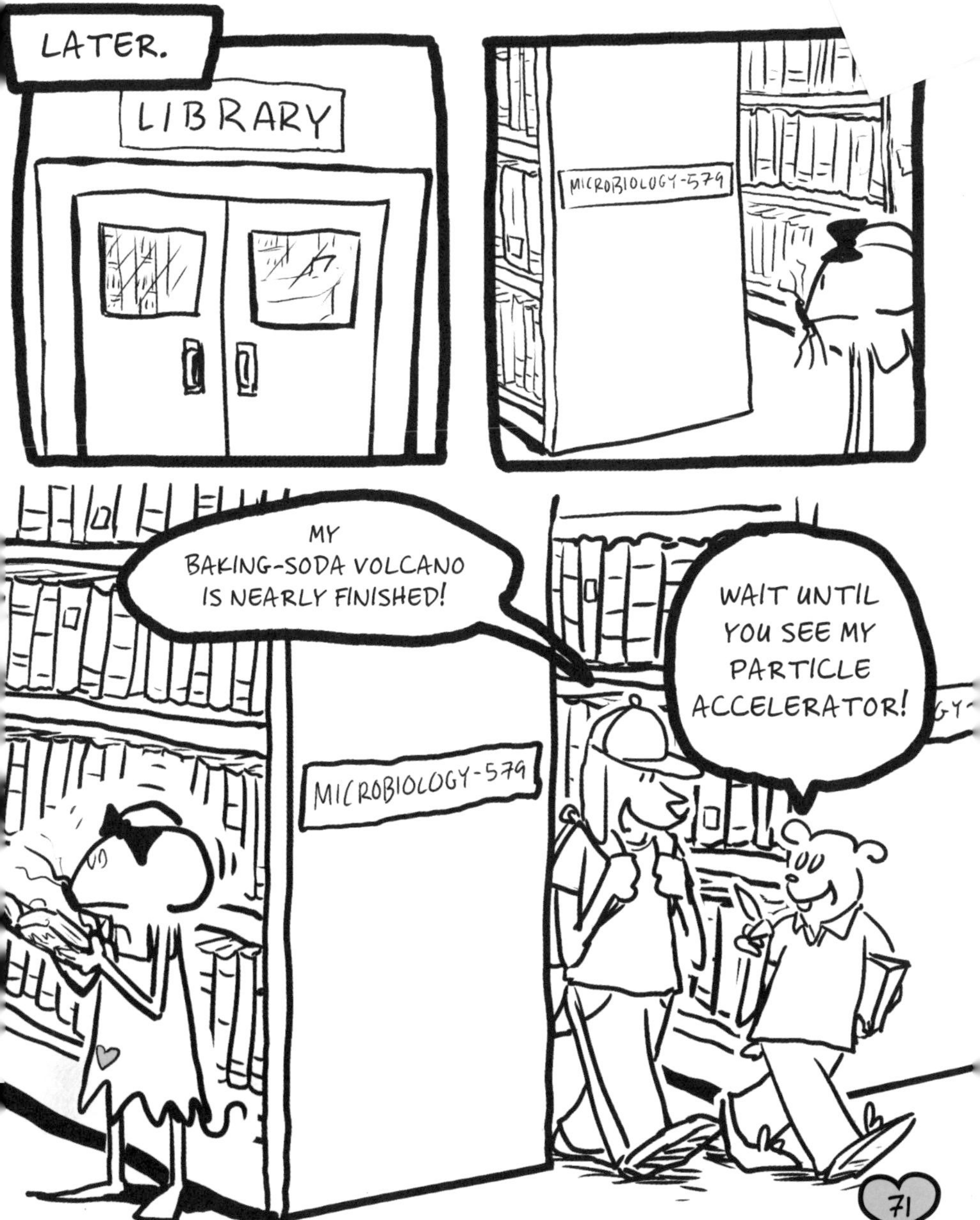
LATER.
LIBRARY
MICROBIOLOGY-579
MICROBIOLOGY-579
MY BAKING-SODA VOLCANO IS NEARLY FINISHED!
WAIT UNTIL YOU SEE MY PARTICLE ACCELERATOR!

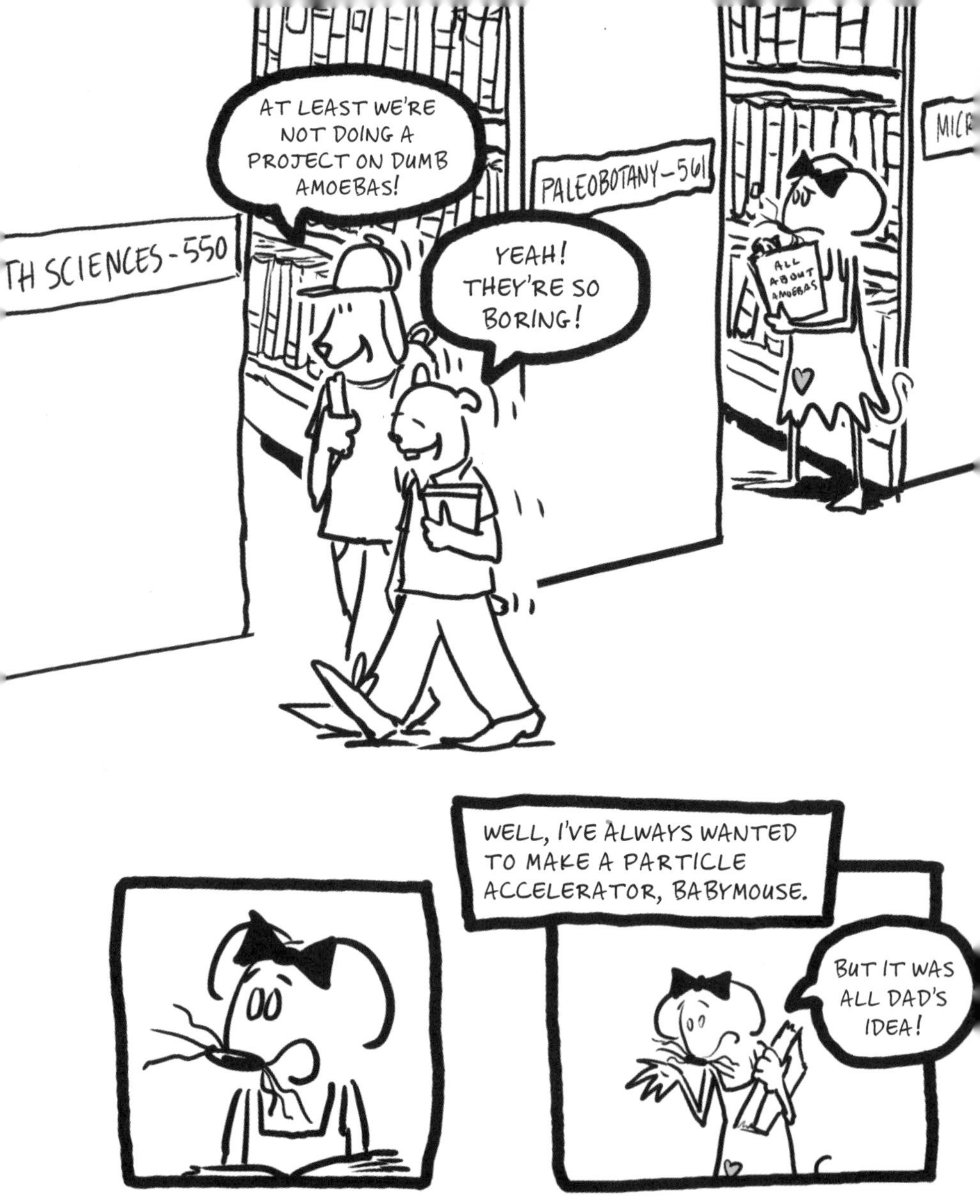

TH SCIENCES - 550
PALEOBOTANY - 561
MICR
AT LEAST WE'RE NOT DOING A PROJECT ON DUMB AMOEBAS!
YEAH! THEY'RE SO BORING!
ALL ABOUT AMOEBAS
WELL, I'VE ALWAYS WANTED TO MAKE A PARTICLE ACCELERATOR, BABYMOUSE.
BUT IT WAS ALL DAD'S IDEA!

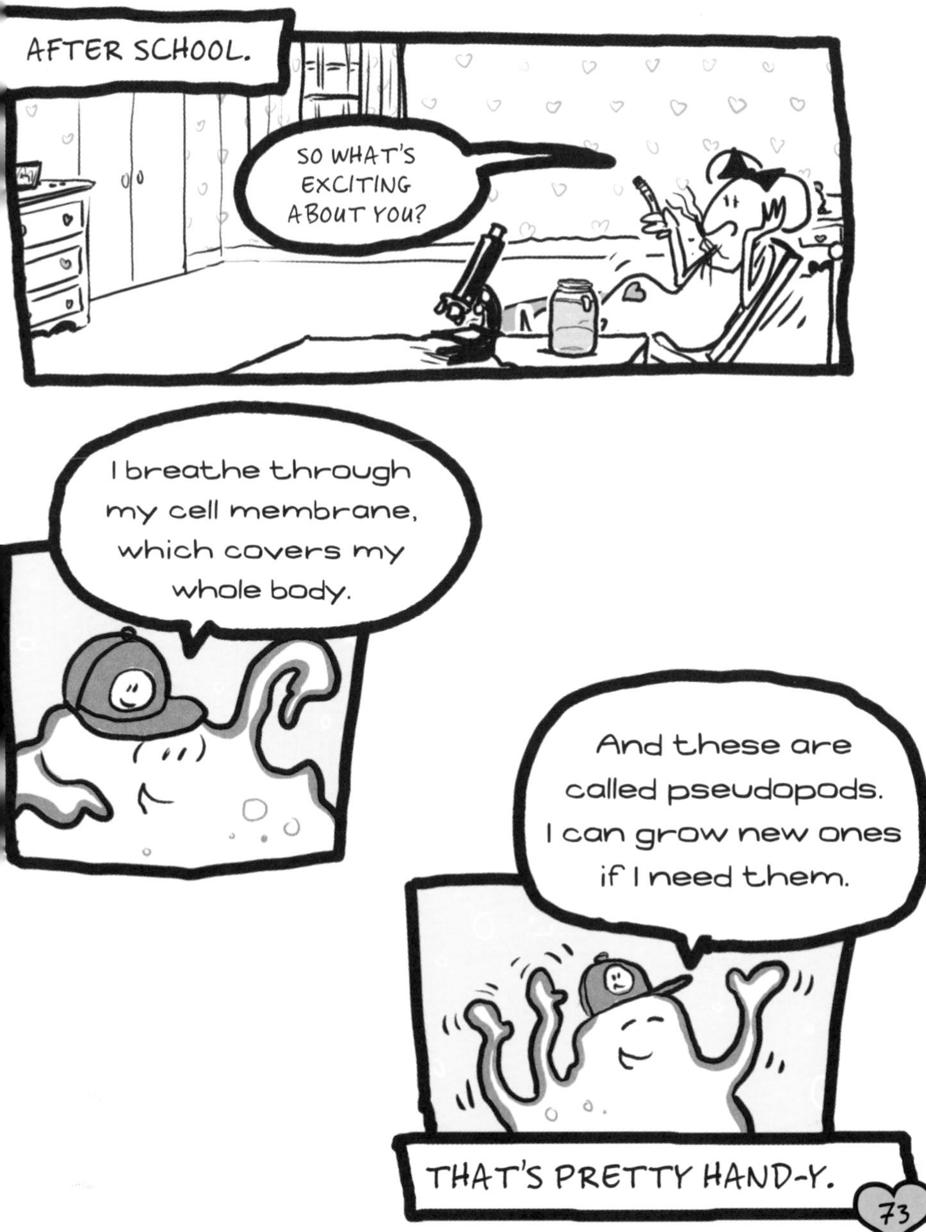
AFTER SCHOOL.
SO WHAT'S EXCITING ABOUT YOU?
I breathe through my cell membrane, which covers my whole body.
And these are called pseudopods. I can grow new ones if I need them.
THAT'S PRETTY HAND-Y.

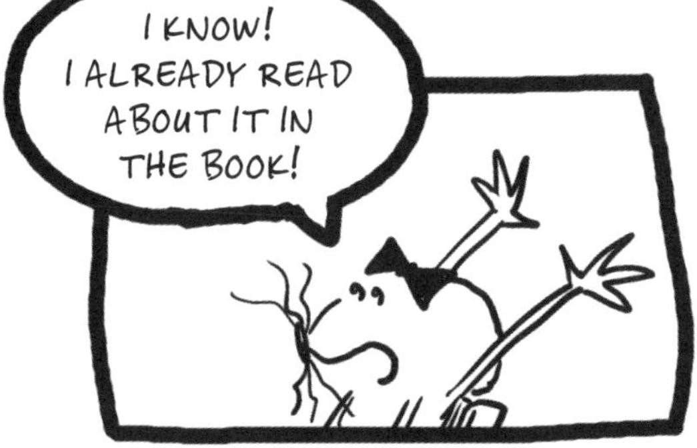
I KNOW! I ALREADY READ ABOUT IT IN THE BOOK!

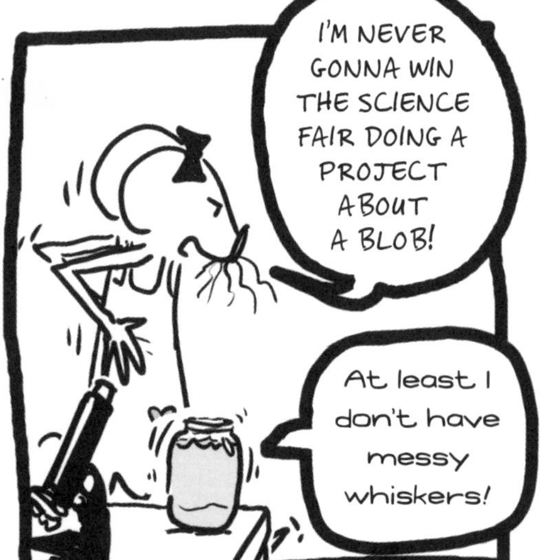
I'M NEVER GONNA WIN THE SCIENCE FAIR DOING A PROJECT ABOUT A BLOB!
At least I don't have messy whiskers!

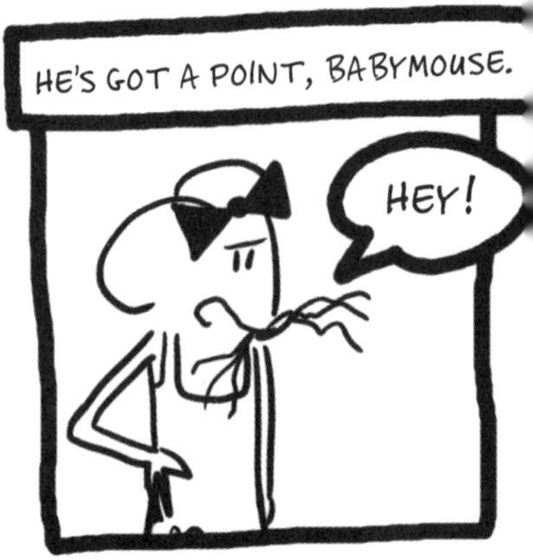
HE'S GOT A POINT, BABYMOUSE.
HEY!

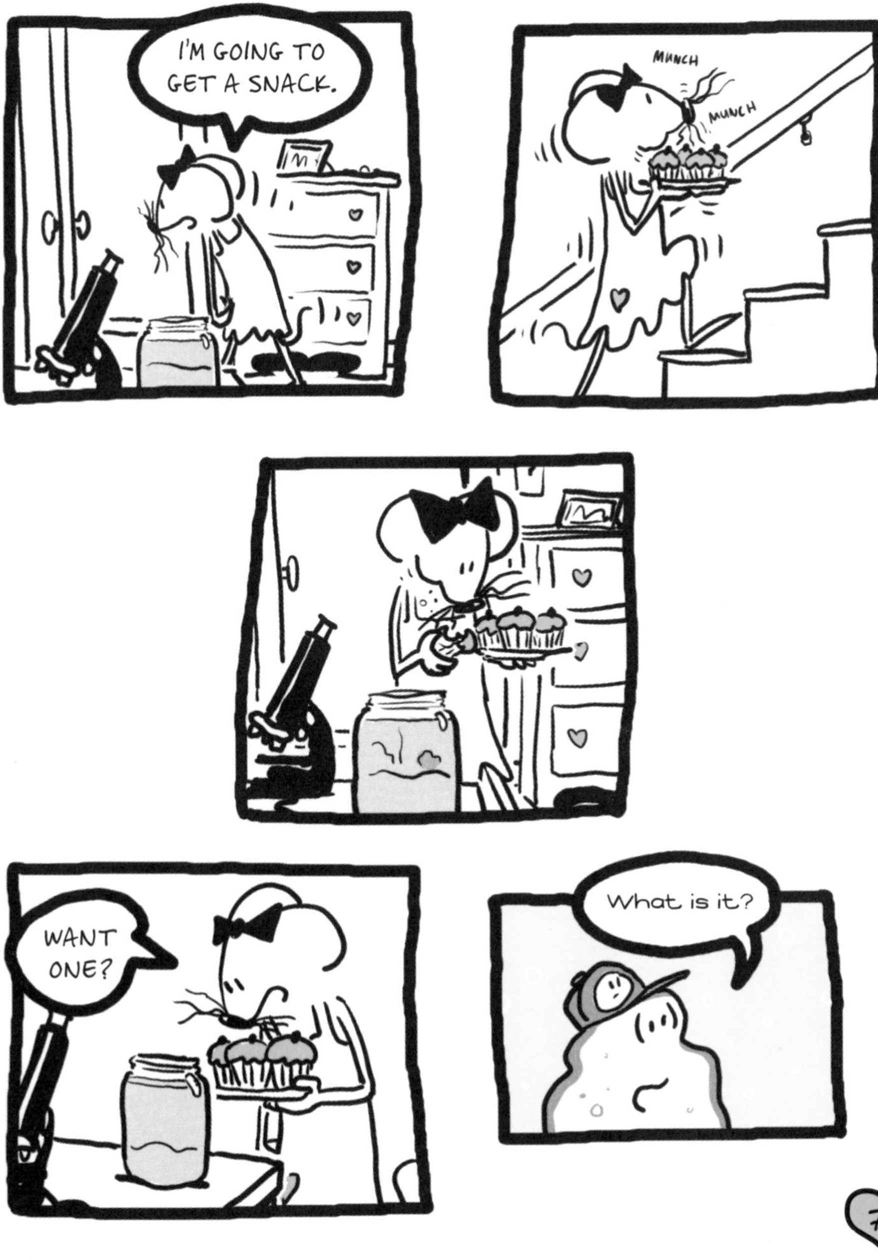
I'M GOING TO GET A SNACK.
MUNCH
MUNCH
WANT ONE?
What is it?

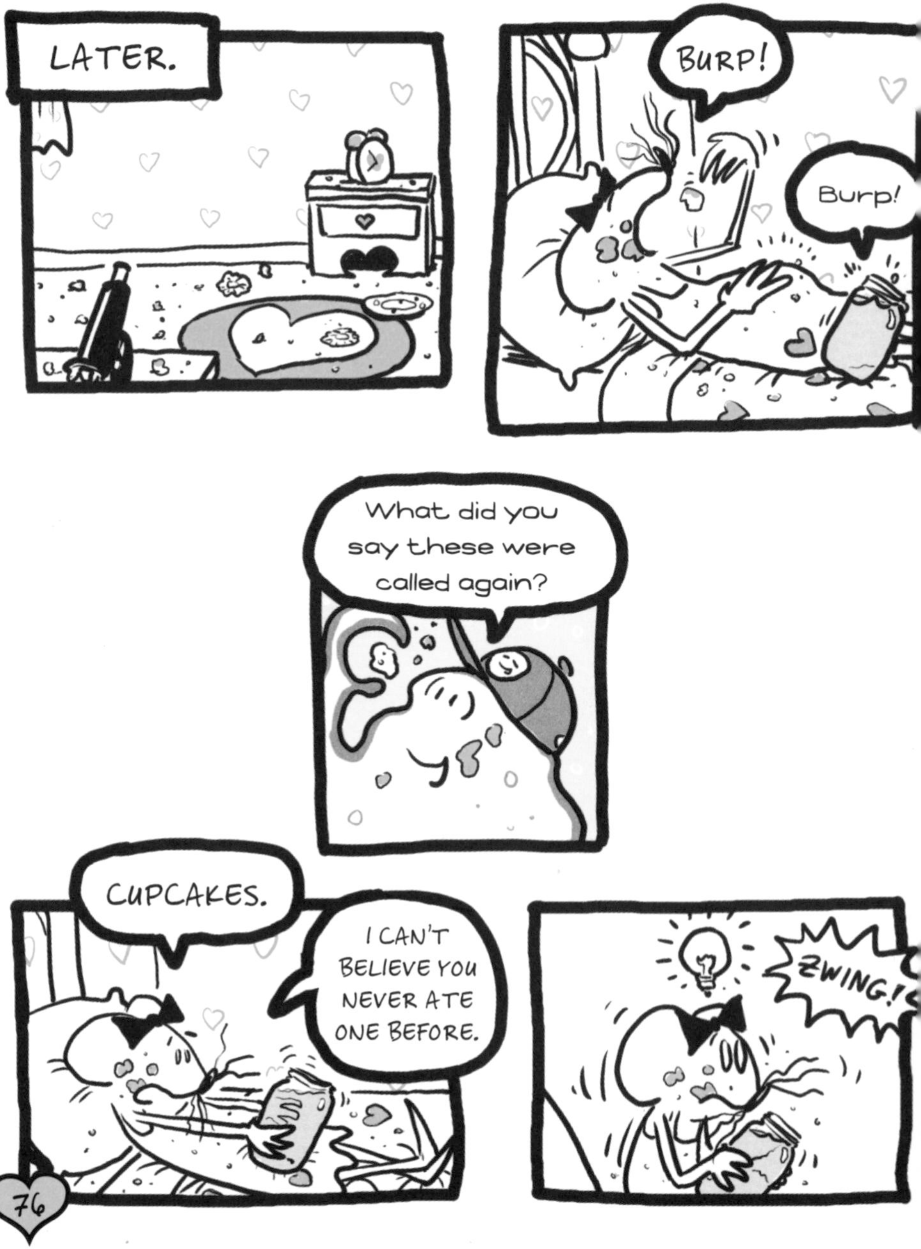
LATER.
BURP!
Burp!
What did you say these were called again?
CUPCAKES.
I CAN'T BELIEVE YOU NEVER ATE ONE BEFORE.
ZWING!

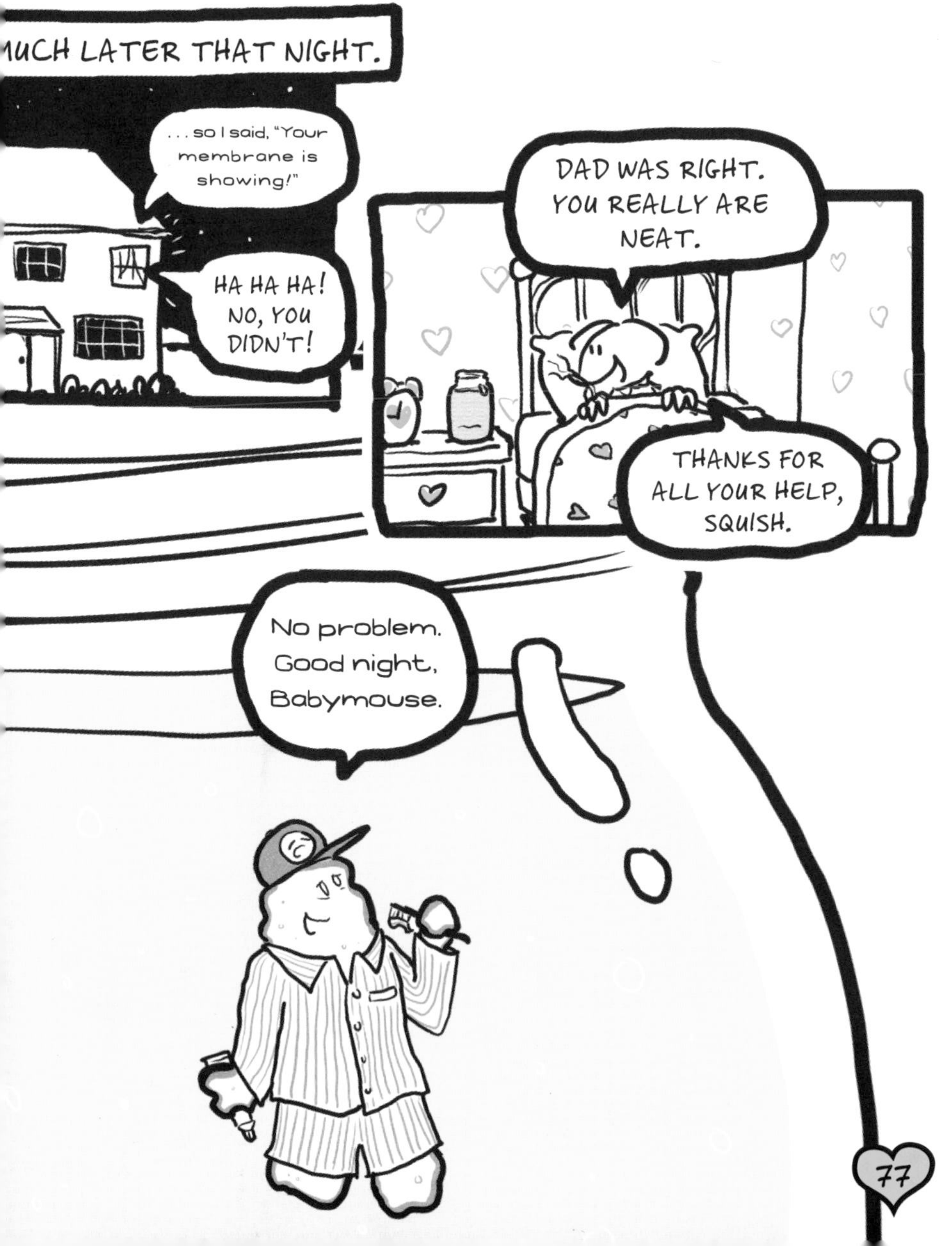

MUCH LATER THAT NIGHT.
. . . so I said, "Your membrane is showing!"
HA HA HA! NO, YOU DIDN'T!
DAD WAS RIGHT. YOU REALLY ARE NEAT.
THANKS FOR ALL YOUR HELP, SQUISH.
No problem. Good night, Babymouse.

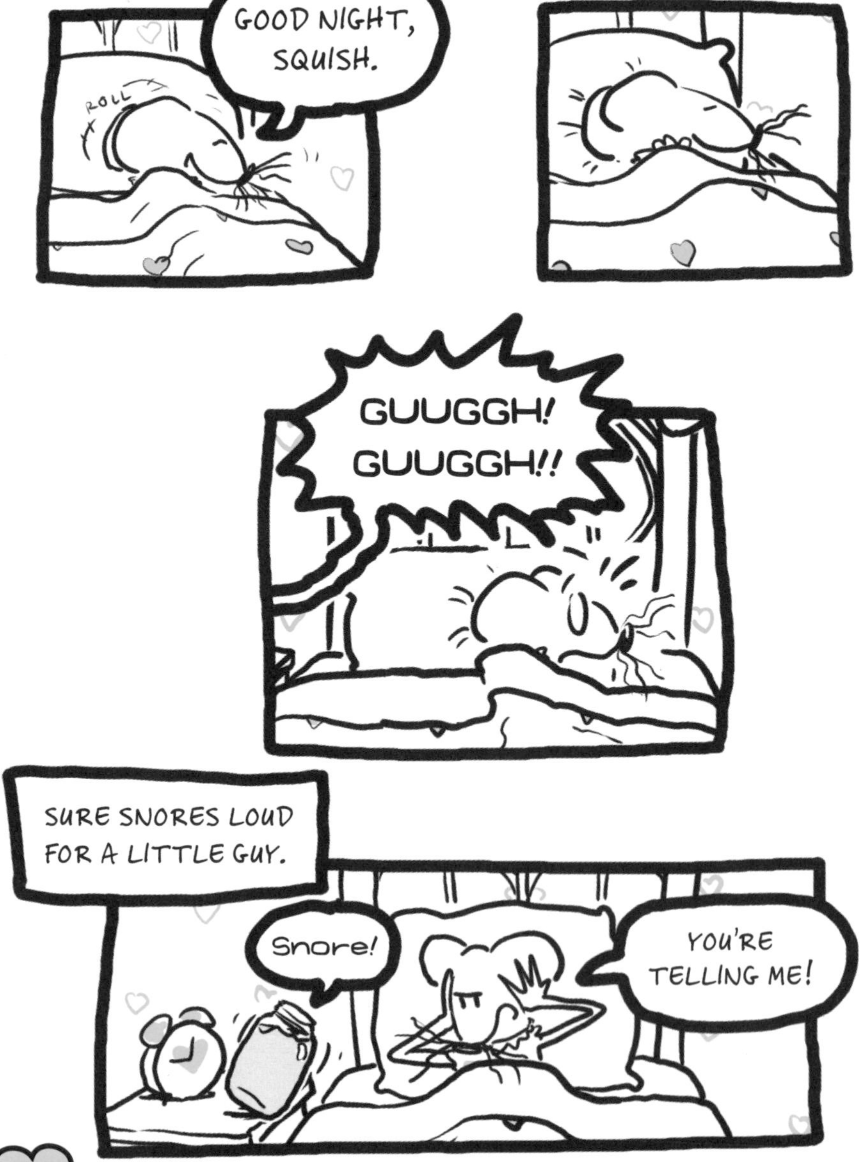
GOOD NIGHT, SQUISH.
ROLL
GUUGGH! GUUGGH!!
SURE SNORES LOUD FOR A LITTLE GUY.
Snore!
YOU'RE TELLING ME!

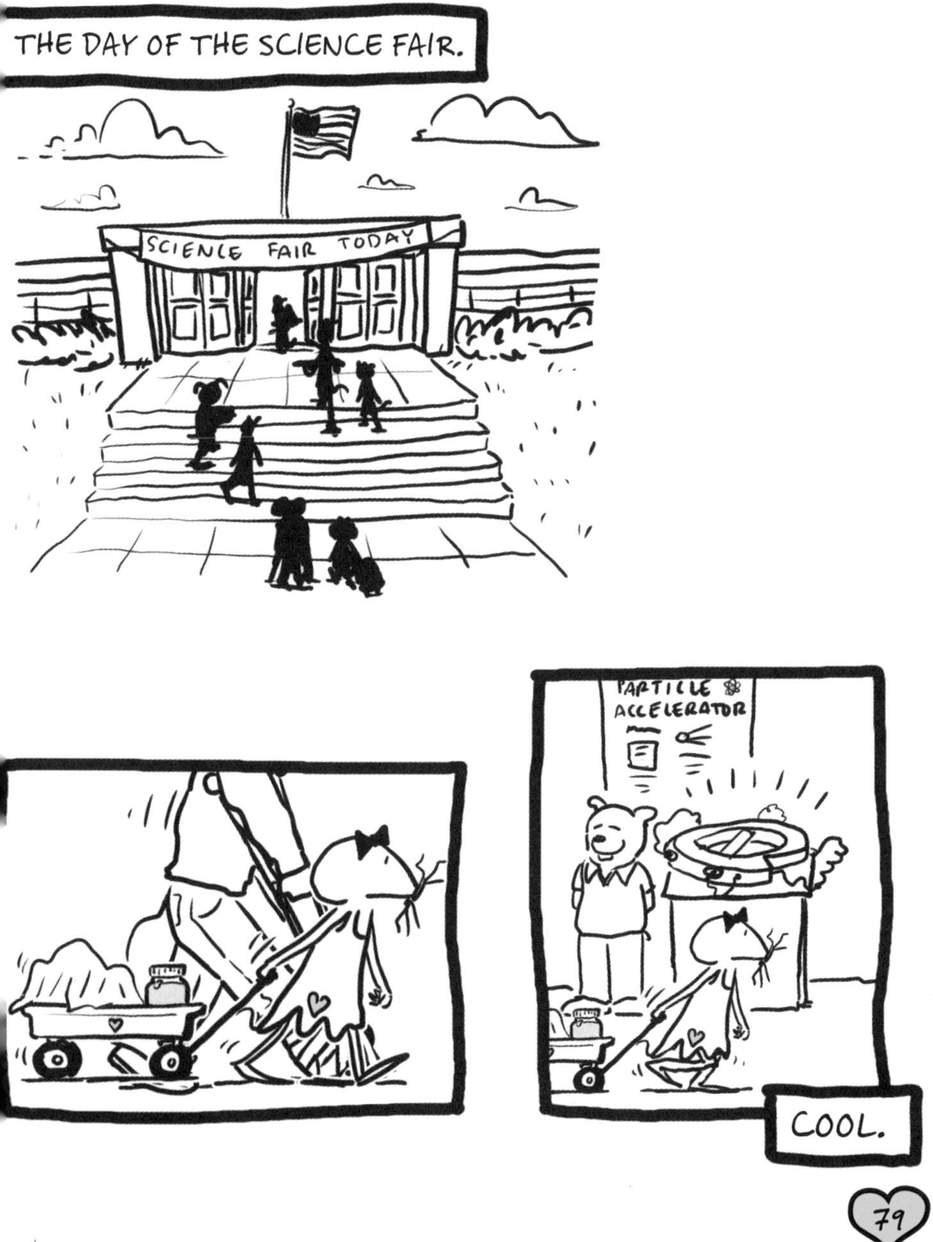
THE DAY OF THE SCIENCE FAIR.
SCIENCE FAIR TODAY
PARTICLE ACCELERATOR
COOL.

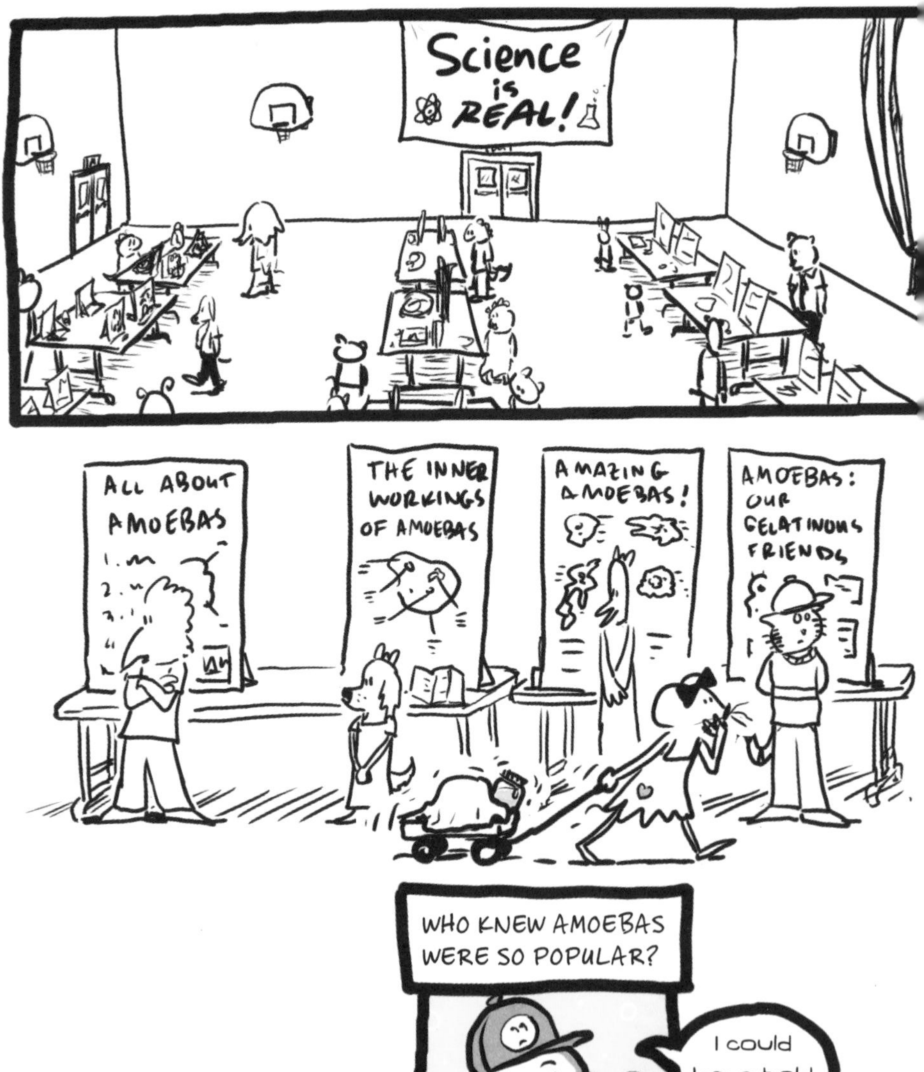
Science is REAL!
ALL ABOUT AMOEBAS
THE INNER WORKINGS OF AMOEBAS
AMAZING AMOEBAS!
AMOEBAS: OUR GELATINOUS FRIENDS
WHO KNEW AMOEBAS WERE SO POPULAR?
I could have told you!